SHEIL

THE HR SUITE

AT ERIE TECHNICAL

TATE PUBLISHING
AND ENTERPRISES, LLC

The HR Suite

Published by Tate Publishing & Enterprises, LLC
127 E. Trade Center Terrace | Mustang, Oklahoma 73064 USA
1.888.361.9473 | www.tatepublishing.com

Tate Publishing is committed to excellence in the publishing industry. The company reflects the philosophy established by the founders, based on Psalm 68:11,
"The Lord gave the word and great was the company of those who published it."

Cover design by Matias Alasagas
Interior design by Nathan Harmony

Published in the United States of America

ISBN: 978-1-62147-505-7
1. Fiction / General
2. Fiction / Contemporary Women
12.10.15

PREFACE

A special thank you to: my mother for always exemplifying and instilling values in me. To: my late father who was the hardest working man that I've known, but was always fun-loving and present in his children's lives. To my beloved son and granddaughter, always have faith (II Cor. 5:7 KJV) and believe in yourself, and do, and be the best person you know how. Finally, thank God for abundantly blessing me and allowing me to complete this project.

PROLOGUE

Although this book is fiction, it all could be true.

I would like for you to meet Carla Blackstone. She is a single Human Resource professional. But both her work life and personal life are filled with twists and turns. She is confronted with issues related to lies, deceit, violence, infidelity, sexuality, suicide, betrayal, and drugs to name a few.

In addition to those that Carla Blackstone will encounter, here are just some of the things HR professionals deal with: disgruntled line employees—upset with management or another employee; management—some feeling that they are superior or right by default in all situations; federal and state laws—constantly changing; domestic violence—things that happen at home flow into the workplace; threats—after layoffs, downsizing or terminations; grief and bereavement—of employees or employee family members; drugs and alcohol—yes functioning drug addicts and alcoholics are employed; serious medical conditions—of all kinds; confidentiality—in all areas and all levels; safety issues—building, air, fire; and pornography—computers violations, just to name a few.

How prepared is your company? And how are these situations handled at your company?

No matter what the economic condition, most of the population is employed. When you watch the tragedies on the news and there is a tragedy, on a daily basis. Most likely the perpetrator is somehow connected to a place of employment. They worked somewhere, or in the case of students, they went to school somewhere. In all cases a Human Resources professional will be involved in some fashion. It may be providing additional security, working with families receiving life insurance, providing bereavement counseling for employees and/or students, or actually being in the midst of the tragedy.

They are the *others* who are tasked to *serve and protect*, but who will protect them?

HR Professionals also have personal lives where they themselves deal with issues like everyone else.

CHAPTER 1

CHARLOTTE, NC. – FALL, 2004

It was a dreary fall evening. The air was thick, and there had been a slow but steady, drizzling rain all day. Carla Blackstone was driving home from another exhausting day at work. As she was driving and talking on her cell phone with a colleague about how they were going to handle an incident at work the following day, all of a sudden she heard a loud thud. She stopped suddenly, shouting "What was that?"

Thomas Benson her colleague on the other line said, "That was my safety binder—it fell from my shelf."

What a relief, Carla thought. The sound seemed so close she could have sworn that it had not come through the phone. "I thought that you said that you hadn't made it home yet," Carla said to Tom. Carla could barely hear him over the sound of barking dogs.

Tom said that he had to go because the sound had frightened his dogs and that he would have to call her back later. When Carla got off of the phone she heard more dogs barking. *It must be a dog-eat-dog night,* she thought as she turned her music back up and continued home.

• • •

Carla was twenty-nine years old and single. She drove a silver Mercedes C-Class. She had wanted the two-seater model. Even though she didn't have any children and rarely had passengers, she thought that it would be selfish, so she couldn't bring herself to get it. Carla was classy yet simple.

Carla only worked for one company since she graduated from college, Erie Technical. Her first position was as an HR assistant. She was very smart and always read journals staying up-to-date on all of the changing rules and regulations in addition to asking questions. After about two years on the job and company growth, Carla was promoted to Human Resource Generalist. She took advantage of the company tuition reimbursement program and worked on her master's degree in business in the evenings over the next three years. Shortly after completing school, the position for HR Manager became available, and of course Carla was a shoe in. She reported to the Vice President of Human Resources Pete Carson. Along the way she had also gotten her PHR (Professional in Human Resources) certification. After two years as Manager, the company continued to grow and a new position was created. She was now Carla Blackstone, Director of Human Resources.

• • •

Tom Benson was one of the only colleagues that Carla felt somewhat close to. Her motto was to never mix business with her personal life and never get too close to anyone at work while in human resources. Tom was thirty-seven years old, married for thirteen years to his wife Carmen. They had two sons—Chance, and Tom Jr.,—and one daughter, Angel.

Tom and Carla had a close relationship because Tom was the building facilities manager and they had to interact quite often on security, safety, and other confidential issues. They knew that they had to work together and trust one another. Most recently Tom seemed to have reasons to leave work early or come in late, which was uncharacteristic of him. Carla had joked with him about his change in behavior because she was concerned, but Tom seemed to take it as a joke so Carla became less concerned.

Although Carla was very popular and social when in the presence of family, friends, and colleagues she genuinely preferred being alone. She rarely initiated outings or visits to family or friends. She felt if she interacted with more people, it would result in unwanted drama. People were complicated and other than as it related to work, Carla didn't want to figure them out. She also never seemed to have a male in her life for long periods of time. Most recently she had dated or thought she dated a guy named Jay who initially called her every day and wanted to see her. He would call her so she could meet him here or there. He never came to pick her up. This bothered Carla, but he introduced her to all of his friends, so she thought this meant that he really liked her. After all, he told her that he loved her many times. He constantly made promises to go on trips or other special outings with her, but always had to cancel for some reason or another. She would get tired of this thinking something must be wrong, but then all of a sudden he would do something really nice for her, so she fell deeper in love with Jay, but nothing changed. He always made it seem like he had been burned in the past and was testing her before he would let her all the way into his life. This went on for almost a year, and finally he stopped calling Carla for no apparent reason.

Carla was hurt and couldn't believe that someone as smart as her had allowed this to go on so long. She put her head back on straight and moved on.

CHAPTER 2

Erie Technical had approximately 800 employees, 200 of which were located at branch offices, and a human resource staff of eight. The HR Suite was located in a secure area on the first floor of a five story building.

In the HR Suite, an employee named Phyllis Jacobs entered and asked to speak to Carla. She had heard that Carla could be trusted.

Stacy greeted Phyllis when she came into the HR Suite. "Can I help you?"

"Yes, I would like to speak with Ms. Blackstone," Phyllis said.

"Is it something that I can assist you with? My name is Stacy Peterson and I am the HR Generalist. I would be happy to help you. I believe that Ms. Blackstone may be busy right now."

"Listen, I have to speak to her and her only. It is very important and I have to speak with her today!" Phyllis replied.

Stacy could tell that it must have been really important by the desperate look on Phyllis's face. "Your name please," Stacy asked.

"Phyllis Jacobs, please tell her that it is urgent."

"Okay Phyllis, I am sure that she will see you. Have a seat and I will let her know that you are here."

Stacy knew that Carla would see her, but practiced the habit of weeding out the employees that she could handle.

"Carla, there is an employee here by the name of Phyllis Jacobs who wants to see you. I tried to see if she would see me, but she insists on seeing you. I do not know what it is about but she says that it is urgent. From my experience and the look on her face I believe that it is," Stacy explained.

"Okay, I was just finishing up my report for Pete. You can bring her in."

"Okay, I will make sure that you are not disturbed, and I will stay close by if you need me." Stacy stepped out into the hallway and signaled for Ms. Jacobs to come to Carla's office.

Carla greeted Phyllis and motioned for her to have a seat. She had spoken to her a few years ago about something but could not remember the particulars.

"How can I help you Phyllis?"

Phyllis took a deep breath and said, "I am afraid. I think that my husband is really going to kill me and I am terrified of him." Carla immediately believed her based on her expression and the trembling in her voice.

"Why do you believe this Phyllis, Carla inquired?"

"We have been having a lot of problems at home that I would not like to discuss, but he told me that he would kill me, so I left and moved in with his mom because I do not have any relatives in the area. She only lives down the street from here. He loves his mom and would never let her know how violent he can be. I feel safe staying there and she is like a mom to me. The problem is he has been calling me here at work and threatening to come here."

"Have you gotten a court order to keep him away from you?"

"Yes, I have it right here. I thought that you might need it," Phyllis said. She broke down in tears trembling several times just trying to get these few words out. What Phyllis didn't know was that her story was not much different than many others Carla had heard before.

With the court order Carla could make arrangements for Phyllis to park out front close to the building as long as the court order was in effect. This made Phyllis feel better. Carla also requested a picture of Phyllis's husband and the make, model, year and color of any vehicle he may be driving. Carla offered her security services that would walk her to her car at the end of the day since it was fall and dark by the time work ended. Carla would have to share some of this information with Tom since he was the primary authority over security. "Ok Phyllis, if you think of any addition information that you think we may need please let me know. I will be back in contact with you this afternoon to explain how it will all work. We will be able to start having security escort you to your car this evening."

Tom was also in charge of the surveillance cameras. Although they were friends, Tom hated it when Carla kept details from him, but Carla would only share the *need to know* information with him. She was a *by the rules and regulations* HR professional. She also needed to share this information with Pete, the company lawyer, and the company president. They were the *need to knows* in this situation. Early in the conversation, she had explained to Phyllis that the conversation would be kept confidential, but a few people in the company would need to know for the safety of all employees. In these situations there was always a meeting of the *need to knows* to come up with a strategy that was suitable to the company president. He rarely involved himself. He just wanted to know that it was being handled in the best interest of the employees and the company. It just happened to be time to start a training series, so now was no better time to make sure that it included the topic of violence in the workplace.

• • •

Later that same day when Carla was exiting the Human Resources Suite, she noticed a handsome young man standing at the security desk. She smiled and said hello to him and proceeded to the ladies' room. On her way back to the HR Suite, she noticed that he hadn't been helped, so she asked if she could help him. He said that he was there to meet his mom, Debra Freeman, for lunch. Carla had him sign in, have a seat and told him that she would call his mom down. She motioned to the guard, who was still on the phone, letting him know that she had handled the situation. She was going to find out later why this young man had been standing there for so long. Carla did small things like this when she noticed something needed to be done. She didn't want there to be a perception that anyone coming to visit Erie Technical was not important. Everyone was a customer in her eyes. The other reason was, although the guard services reported directly to Tom, they indirectly reported to Pete on the organization chart and Pete had delegated this responsibility to Carla. Carla used the lobby phone to call the young man's mother and told him that she would be right down. He very politely smiled and thanked her. As Carla walked back to her office, she turned again to look at the young man. He looked to be about thirteen. She felt like she had seen him before, but just couldn't place where.

• • •

After lunch, an employee, that Carla didn't really know but had seen in passing, stopped by Pete Carson's office to have a word with him about Carla. After the meeting, Pete called Carla to his office to explain their strange exchange. He said, "An employee by the name of Debra Freeman wanted to know why you called her when her son stopped by, instead of the security officer at the front desk." Pete said that he explained to Ms. Freeman that the security staff reported to both Carla and Tom, and that Carla was just making sure that visitors weren't waiting long in the lobby without being taken care of. He said that Ms. Freeman still seemed to have a problem with it even though he had explained that it was not an unusual event.

Carla thought that it was strange too, but so were a lot of other things. She didn't know this particular employee, so she knew that she had not been involved in any employee relation issues. Pete seemed to think that maybe they knew each other and had a past, but Carla assured him that wasn't the case. *This was just another day at the OK Erie Corral*, Carla thought, but for some reason, she loved it.

CHAPTER 3

The workforce at Erie Technical was very diverse in cultures, religions, ethnic backgrounds, and lifestyles. Patricia Montgomery, or Pat, as she was called, was gay. Pat came by one day to discuss a situation that she was having. She had come to feel close to Carla because on many occasions their departments had to work closely together. Carla thought that she was cool too. Pat confided in Carla that her work production was being effected by a personal problem she was struggling with at work. This was uncharacteristic of Pat. She was known to always be on top of her game. She was well-respected for her skills. She ran the IT Department. Carla already knew that Pat had a long-time partner. They had met at a few company events, and on occasion, when one of their cars was in the shop. Pat's partner would drop her off in front of the building, outside of Carla's window.

Pat confided in Carla that she felt she was falling in love with someone else at work. She said that she didn't want to divulge who it was, but that the person was in management, and she too felt like Carla—that business should be kept separate from personal life. Pat had to work very close with many department heads. Carla didn't know who she was referring to nor did she want to know. Nevertheless, Pat opened up that it had gotten so bad that in an argument with her partner it had come up. She didn't want to hurt her partner's feelings but had done so by continuously bringing up this person's name, for which she was infatuated with. Now she was struggling at home, because her partner had become jealous and wanted her to find another job.

What her partner didn't know was that if Pat found another job, that she would definitely approach this person. The work relationship was the only thing that was stopping her. She admitted that she was fantasizing about being with this person. In the end Carla suggested that Pat utilize the Employee Assistance

Program (EAP). This was a company-sponsored, confidential, free benefit that offered counseling.

• • •

It wasn't unusual for an employee to be sitting in the lobby when Carla came to work in the mornings. There was a third shift, so sometimes an employee or two were in the lobby, waiting for a ride. Carla walked past a young man, spoke, and unlocked the door to the Suite. It was still an hour before the official opening of business, so Carla was about to lock the door behind her, when Jeffrey walked up and introduced himself as a third-shift employee that had been waiting an hour already to get to speak to her. Even though Carla did not know him personally she knew all the employees' names just by coming across them through the new hire process, annual reviews, disciplinary action, or the HRIS system (Human Resource Information System). Now she knew the face that went with the name, Jeffery Jordon. Jeffery was about twenty-five and wanted to know if he had a child out of wedlock and did not live in the same household with the mother, whether he would be able to cover the child on his medical insurance. He seemed to be excited. He said that he couldn't marry his girlfriend yet, but that he planned to do so after the baby was born. Carla congratulated him, and told him that the child could be covered and that he had plenty of time to take care of things, since his girlfriend just found out that she was only six weeks pregnant. Carla suggested that he contact the Benefits Specialist and that there were regulations that did have a time limit to get the baby covered after he or she was born.

CHAPTER 4

Hiring a new employee required getting the position approved, choosing the best strategy to recruit for a particular position, advertising, weeding through tons of resumes, telephone screens, setting up interviews, negotiating salaries, and sending out offer letters, contingent upon the result of drug and criminal background checks. Of course, when you first secure the services of drug and background check companies, you have to review several proposals and sit through tons of presentations. Jonathan Davis had convinced Stacy that he really needed to start working, so she requested that he start before his background check came back. This was unusual for the company, but not unheard of. The company was covered because the offer was contingent upon the results of the background check.

When the criminal background check came back, Stacy rushed to Carla's office to tell her that there was a problem. Carla requested Jonathan's employee file for review. The first thing she searched for was to see if they had missed the fact that he had indicated he had been convicted of a felony on his application. When a background check indicated criminal history, Carla or Pete always contacted the potential candidate to ask for details of what had occurred. This was done because employers cannot discriminate against someone because they had a conviction. They had to make an informed decision based on the crime, the nature of the business, and other factors. After reviewing the application, Carla felt somewhat relieved. Mr. Davis had checked that he had never been convicted of a felony. Now it would be easier to dismiss him for falsifying his application.

• • •

Normally a manager was responsible for terminations, but in cases like this, Human Resources handled the process. Stacy did not feel comfortable firing him, so

Carla coached her and told her that she would sit in with her. Carla had dealt with numerous uncomfortable situations and felt that it was important for her staff to learn to do the same. Carla contacted Tom; he needed to be aware, in case they encountered a security issue.

• • •

When Mr. Davis entered Stacy's office and saw Carla with Stacy, he knew something was wrong. They allowed him to sit closest to the door. This was a practice, in case the person was angry and wanted to leave. This method made for less of a possibility of anyone getting hurt, having obstacles or anyone between the terminated employee and the door. Stacy told Mr. Davis that unfortunately because he neglected to state that he had a criminal background that it was considered *falsification of application* and that his employment would have to be terminated.

Mr. Davis pleaded for his job and explained that everyone he knew had advised him that if he would have indicated that he had a conviction, he would not be hired. He said that he wanted to tell the truth but just made a bad decision. He kept saying that he did his time and should not have to be punished forever. He began to cry. It was one of the most uneasy situations Carla had been involved in. She hated to see a grown man cry. She also believed that once a felon did his/her time, that they deserved fair treatment. The problem here was that he had lied. Then all of a sudden, he started to blame Carla. He felt a connection to Stacy because she had let him start early. He did not feel the same for Carla. He thought Stacy was being forced to do this because of Carla. He kept telling Carla that she could make an exception for him.

Carla told him that it was consistent with what they had done every time in the past. She told him that if he would have openly divulged the fact that he had a conviction he may have still been hired. She told him that they have other employees with a criminal past, but in all cases they had indicated such on their applications.

It was taking too long, and Stacy was not bringing closure to the conversation, so Carla told Mr. Davis that she was sorry, but that they had to be consistent and that the decision would not change, and wished him the best as she stood to signal that the meeting was over. Mr. Davis thanked Stacy for giving him a chance. As he was leaving his head hung low and under his breath he said, "You'll get yours," directed at Carla. This made Carla feel uncomfortable because she really did feel for him and was just following the rules. When things like this occurred she sometimes wished that she was married and didn't have to be home alone. She would get a little paranoid after situations like that and take extra precautions driving home and locking her doors. As an HR professional, she didn't want any of the employees to know where she lived and that was exactly why.

CHAPTER 5

Dale Carson, an African American male with a visible handicap felt that he deserved a pay increase and came down to Human Resources to complain about his manager. He claimed that she was discriminating against him because she wouldn't give him an increase. Carla asked Stacy to handle this one. Stacy had to consult with Carla any time there was an employee relations issue that involved anything that could have potential legal implications, and Carla had to run it by Pete. Since Dale claimed discrimination, this was a situation that would have to come back to her anyway. Stacy knew that the first rule of thumb was that she had to make an appointment with Dale right away.

• • •

Phyllis Jacobs called Carla to say that she couldn't get any work done because her husband kept calling and threatening her, and she had to answer her phone as a part of her job. Changing her number was not an option, because most of the time customers called the operator and were transferred. Carla contacted Pat Montgomery in IT, who was in charge of telecommunications as well, and asked her to run a report for the past week on all incoming calls to Phyllis Jacobs. After receiving the report, to her surprise, he had called Phyllis an average of thirty times per day.

Carla and her boss Pete met with the company attorney who suggested that Phyllis should contact the police, because of the harassment at work since she already had a court order, and that the company would share the telephone report with them if necessary. In the meantime, Phyllis's calls were forwarded to Human Resources. They took the calls and forwarded legitimate customers to her that had account numbers. Her husband continued calling, and they would say that she wasn't available. Finally, Carla took one of his calls and told him that he couldn't keep calling Phyllis at work because he was disrupting business. She told him that they had records of his calls, that it was considered harassment, and to please stop calling. He cursed at Carla and hung up. Human Resources continued to take Phyllis's calls for the next two days and no other calls had come in from him, so calls were transferred back to Phyllis. Phyllis was very thankful.

• • •

Carla loved home cooking and very rarely went to restaurants, but today was an exception. She had had a rough day. It was time for benefits' open enrollment, performance appraisals were just completed, and various year-end projects were almost due, along with the holidays. As she was leaving work, she ran into Pat and Tom.

Although Pat and Tom were Carla's closest colleagues, she didn't believe in hanging out with them or any other colleague after work hours. She made the mistake of saying that she was starving and was about to grab a bite to eat. Of course they were about to do the same and pressed Carla to join them. Carla gave in with the promise that work would not be discussed.

As she followed in her car, she wanted to come up with an excuse as to why she needed to rush home to take care of something, but couldn't come up with a good excuse. Carla hated lying. As a matter of fact, she couldn't remember when she last told a *true lie*. When she made excuses, there had to be some truth in it. Carla strongly believed that when you told a lie you only cause unwanted stress for yourself and you would just end up having to tell another lie. She was pretty good at saying no or being truthful and avoided doing things that she really didn't want to.

As they pulled up to TGI Friday's, Carla thought of a legitimate excuse as to why she wouldn't stay long. Everyone knew that she was an adamant sports fan, and it was both basketball and football season, so she would need to get home in time to settle in for a game. As they were ordering, Pat's phone rang, and it was her partner Le'ann. Pat didn't seem so happy to hear from her; when she got off the phone, she let them know that Le'ann would be joining them.

Carla said, "great." At least she was someone Carla didn't work with. She liked Le'ann based on their few encounters. Carla ordered a glass of strawberry lemonade. Both Pat and Tom ordered stiffer drinks.

Just before they were served their meals, Le'ann showed up. She seemed very surprised to see Tom and Carla. Thinking back, Pat never said that anyone was with her. Le'ann kissed Pat and then was overly friendly to both Tom and Carla. This behavior made Carla remember that they were having problems and that she was probably trying to do the extras to keep Pat, since it was Pat that had feelings for someone else. They never discussed the job and as a result, Carla was okay with this outing.

As soon as Carla finished eating, she happily excused herself and left her share of the tab and a generous tip. As she drove home, she felt good as she always did when she (once in a blue moon) participated in anything with anyone from work. She had survived. No one else from work had been at TGI Friday's and there was no shop talk.

When Carla pulled up in front of her house, she finished listening to the song that was on the radio. She loved music. Although she couldn't sing a lick, when she was in her car or in the shower, it was as if she were in a music studio. She sang loud and with feeling, never hitting a tune. For some reason when she put her key in the door it felt like someone was looking at her and it made her feel uncomfortable, so she hurried in and locked the door behind her as she always did. This time she decided to look out the window before she turned on the lights to see if she saw anyone.

A couple of cars went by, but nothing unusual. Carla thought, *What a chicken I can be sometimes.* Then she turned the lights on and went on about her nightly routine, except for preparing herself something to eat. When her phone rang, it startled her for a second, but as usual she didn't answer and let it go to her answering machine.

It was a male voice. It was an old boyfriend. Carla had stayed cordial the few times she saw him in passing after their breakup but didn't want anything to do with him. He pretended to want to be her friend, but she wasn't buying it. She had no intentions of picking up the phone until he said that he was in the neighborhood. She picked up the phone, because she couldn't act like she wasn't home. Knowing him, he had probably already driven by or saw her go in.

He laughed and said, "I see you are still not answering your phone, but I am glad that you picked up for me." He said he thought he would stop by if he could, since he was in the neighborhood and maybe watch Monday Night Football like they use to, no strings attached. *What the hell is he talking about*, Carla thought? *He gave up his right to see me when he cheated*, Carla thought. Rather than being rude, she said that she had had a bad day, had just been out with friends, had a headache and would not be watching football tonight, because she was going to go straight to bed. Carla wanted no beef with anyone so she told him to take care and that she was about to go to bed. When she hung up, she thought, *What makes him think that I ever want to see him again*. She had not called him once in the past three years since she caught him with another woman at his house.

• • •

It had been a Saturday night. Carla had just come from a concert with her childhood friend, Cathy, who was in town on business for the week. After dropping Cathy off, she thought she would stop by his place and surprise him. Through the window she noticed that his lights were on, but dim. When she got to the door she could hear music playing. When she knocked, the music was turned off, and she thought that he was on his way to the door, but there was no answer, so after a few minutes Carla went back to her car to try to figure out what was going on. There wasn't another car in his driveway. Then it dawned on her that she had his house key. She didn't know what to do. She wanted to trust him, but if something was going on she was going to have to bust him. If she didn't, she figured that she would only get the deny version that her male college buddies had told her about. "If you didn't see me, *it wasn't me and I didn't do it.*"

She decided to take the key out of her glove compartment and went back and opened the door. Carla was devastated by what she saw. She threw the key at him and left. There was no need for explanation. It was all spelled out in detail right before her eyes. It was as if a bullet had penetrated her heart.

• • •

After that night Carla had started spending longer hours than normal at work just to keep her mind occupied. She had problems eating and cried a lot when she wasn't at work. As they say time heals all wounds, and Carla finally healed and was not planning to be shot by that bullet again. She wished that she would have just told him that he wasn't welcome to her home anymore but wished him well. Instead her excuse of going to bed didn't make it clear. She promised herself that if he ever contacted her again she would be cordial, but very clear. His call after three years had caught her off guard.

Carla turned off the lights and did go to bed, but not without switching back and forth between the

Dallas Cowboys versus the Washington Redskins and the Miami Heat versus the Boston Celtics. She didn't care if he did drive by and saw her television light on most of the night. She wasn't missing football or basketball to avoid a two-timing bum.

CHAPTER 6

Every morning when Carla got into the office, she would always check her voice mail and e-mails before starting anything else. She only had five messages. *Thank goodness*, she thought. The first was a manager, requesting to discuss a situation about an employee. Carla forwarded that message to Stacy to handle. The next call was a vendor, from a recruiting service. She had recently told them that their services were not needed at that time, so she pressed delete. Then there was another vendor, an insurance broker, and yet another vendor, selling an electronic performance appraisal system. It was wonderful to be able to forward these to Stacy, who was very good in dealing with the numerous vendor calls that were received on a daily basis. Finally, the last call was from an employee in one of the west coast offices.

He said that he was calling from a pay phone, and changing his voice because he wanted to report something very serious going on in the office dealing with illegal drugs. All of sudden there was a loud noise, and the phone went dead. Carla saved that message and then forwarded it to Pete and the company attorney, Garrett Morgan. In her message she requested a time for them to discuss how to handle that call. In the meantime, she had found out that the call did come from an area code on the west coast near where they had an office.

• • •

Later in the morning Carla and Garret met and decided to call the City Director for the San Diego office, Paul Black. Pete had a meeting outside of the office all morning and felt that he could get an update. The call was made from Garrett's office.

"I have Carla Blackstone from Human Resources with me as well," Garrett said.

"Oh no," Paul said to himself, "the company attorney and Human Resources, this can't be good." He tried to sound calm and said, "So what can I do for two of my favorite people?"

"Paul, is there anything, anything whatsoever happening in your office that you believe we should know?" Garrett asked.

Paul was silent for a moment, trying to figure out what this was all about.

Then Carla interjected by saying that they had received some disturbing news that something illegal might be going on in their office and asked if he knew anything about it?

"Now that you mention it, I have been looking into a rumor that has been going around—"

"And what is that?" Garrett asked.

"Well, I was told that some of my employees may be involved in selling drugs, but I haven't been able to verify anything yet."

"How long have you known?" Carla asked.

"For about a month or so," Paul responded.

Garrett interrupted again, partly angry and partly sarcastic, "So when were you going to notify me or Human Resources?"

Paul said he didn't want to bother them with something that may have been nothing.

Carla and Garrett looked at each other in astonishment. They went on to question Paul for another half hour, both taking notes. Then Paul was told to put everything that he knew about the situation in writing and to call Carla when he was finished, so that she could receive his signed statement on the fax confidentially. He was also told not to discuss this call with anyone.

After the call, Carla and Garrett didn't have too much to say, they were both still astonished and agreed to meet again after Paul's statement was received. After reading Paul's statement, Carla began to get a headache. How could Paul be so stupid and potentially have his employees in a knowingly dangerous environment? Who had made him Manager of Drug Investigations? Timing was good because the Regional Director who Paul reported to, had a planned trip to the west coast, so it was decided that Carla should go as well and plan a training class as a cover.

CHAPTER 7

A few days later, Carla was in flight to sunny San Diego, California. *What a pleasure it would be if this were a personal trip*, she thought. Nevertheless, you can always add a little pleasure to any business trip. Maybe she could take a morning jog on the beach or maybe just take a walk along the beach in the evening. Carla loved the ocean. She wasn't really a swimmer and rarely got in the water. One of her favorite things to do, other than listening to music and watching a sporting event, was to admire the beauty of the beach. There was no greater peace or beauty. She would be there for three days, maybe she could get one moment of peace.

• • •

As soon as Carla's plane landed she checked her voice mail. There were four messages, all of which she forwarded to Stacy. This made Carla happy. She didn't like having to escalate things to Pete. She wanted her boss to have faith in her that she could handle the day-to-day issues as well as the not so day-to-day issues.

Carla went to the car rental counter to get her car and directions from the airport to the office. The gentleman assisting her was the cutest, sexiest, piece of candy that she had seen in quite some time. His teeth were pearly white and his smile was captivating. His eyes even seemed to twinkle. *My goodness*, Carla thought. Apparently, he had been trying to hand her the keys when she came out of her daydream. His touch startled her. She guessed his age to be around twenty-two, seven years younger than her. *He had to be immature*, she thought. Carla thought she had better run before she literally melted on the spot. As she walked away she remembered a scene in a movie that she loved. She kept thinking, *is he looking at me while I walk away*? Finally, she got the courage to turn around, and he was. She smiled and waved, then tripped on the old invisible bump. *Oh, grow up before you kill yourself,* she thought, *you are no longer a college freshman getting all giddy over a guy.* Instead of going to check in at her hotel, she headed straight for the office with the directions that Mr. Cutie had given her.

• • •

This was Carla's first time visiting this office. As she pulled up her cell phone rang. "Good morning, this is Carla."

On the other end was Tom Benson. "Hey woman, you didn't tell me that you were leaving town and leaving me here alone to defend the universe."

"I thought I told you that I had to come out here to conduct some training classes." She knew that she had not mentioned it to him. After all, she was on somewhat of an undercover mission. As she was reaching into the backseat for her things, a car pulled up a few spaces from her, and one of the ladies that had been standing outside smoking, walked over and exchanged something with the driver. *That was strange*, Carla thought. It didn't appear that they said a word to one another. Carla told Tom that she had arrived at the office and would call him when she could. He explained that he didn't really want anything and he had just called to harass her.

Carla put on her sunglasses and headed toward the entrance of the building. As she approached, she remembered that an access key card was required. Before she had a chance to make a call, someone coming in held the door for her. *What kind of security is this*, she thought. *He doesn't know me from Jane. I could be the East Coast Daytime Slayer for all he knows.* Carla met with Paul and the Regional Director, who had come out on a different flight the night before for about an hour to discuss their game plan for the following day. After their meeting, she went around the office introducing herself to the many employees. She answered lots of HR related questions. She met the second shift when they came on duty and planned to be in the office early enough in the morning to meet the third shift before they left.

• • •

Around five in the evening, she headed for the hotel. She was tired and starving. After all, her flight had left Charlotte at seven in the morning, and with the time change had arrived in San Diego at ten and had been in the work zone all the while. She checked into her hotel around six. Once she got in her room, she immediately took off her shoes and suit jacket. She was tempted to take a shower and put on something more comfortable, but she was afraid that she would get out of the shower and fall asleep without eating, so she elected to go down to the hotel restaurant for dinner. The restaurant had a live jazz band playing. Oh, how wonderful it was to finally sit back and relax. At home she would have been washing clothes, cleaning, or still at work. She ordered a large chicken Caesar salad.

While waiting for her salad, none other than Mr. Cutie walked up to her table and asked if she remembered him. Of course she remembered, but tried to act as if she had difficulty recalling their encounter. "You're the cand—I mean car rental guy, sure I remember you. What are you doing here?"

"I will tell you if you let me join you."

"Be my guest." Carla smiled. All along she was thinking she should have taken that shower and freshened up for dinner.

"My name is Guy Redding."

"And I am Carla."

"Blackstone," Guy finished for her.

Again Carla asked what he was doing there.

He explained that he knew exactly how to tell her to get to her company office building, because he was working on his PhD and taking a class in the building next to that office. When he saw her leaving the office he couldn't believe his eyes, so he admitted to following her, hoping that she had not eaten and would come down for a bite to eat, and he was right. *Well, he has to be at least twenty-five, four years younger than me, if he is working on his PhD*, Carla thought. His eyes were just mesmerizing to Carla. A few times he had to get her attention. Each time she apologized and claimed she was thinking about a work situation.

The waiter came over to see if Guy needed anything. He asked Carla if she would mind if he ordered and had dinner with her. What could she say? Carla felt great as she swayed a little to the music and was having dinner with a piece of art that belonged in a museum. Imagine a body and smile like LL Cool J, the charm and appeal of Brad Pitt and the natural swagger of Denzel Washington all rolled up in one. Guy was very easy to talk to. Even though she was enjoying herself, work always came first, and she had to get a shower and prepare for an early morning if she was going to meet the third shift. As much as she hated to say it, she told Guy that it was very nice meeting him, but that she had to go.

He asked how long she would be in town and if she wanted to have dinner the next evening that she could give him a call. He gave her his home and cell number. He walked her out and said that he would escort her to her room. As handsome as he was, she knew better than to allow that to happen. She might not be able to control herself. Let's just say very adult thoughts were currently crossing her mind. Besides, she didn't know him from Jack. She declined his offer to escort her upstairs, but told him that she would give him a call for dinner tomorrow if time permitted.

Carla showered and set the alarm clock for five in the morning. She wanted to catch the news but was fast asleep right after she turned the television on.

CHAPTER 8

Carla was up at five having a buffet breakfast at 5:45, and on the road by 6:15. She made it to the office by 6:35. Again, she had forgotten to get access to the building, so she decided to check her voice mails, since she had forgotten to do so after dinner last night. Hopefully, she could catch someone coming in or out again. This time Carla had eight messages. One was from Phyllis Jacobs, saying that she knew that Carla was away, but she needed to talk to her as soon as possible. The next message was from Jeffrey Jordan, who asked her to call him as soon as she could. The others she was able to reply back with answers. She could call Jeffrey back now, because he was on the third shift and would be off work, but she would have to call Phyllis back between her training classes.

As Carla was about to call Jeffrey, the same car that had pulled up when she first got into town yesterday was there again, only this time the driver and a passenger seemed to be scanning the parking lot and made eye contact with her. She decided to dial Jeffrey and get out of the car at the same time, so that it would not appear that she was making a phone call to the police or waiting for something to happen, if in fact something shady was going on. Luckily she got Jeffrey's voice mail, because she would not have been able to concentrate on whatever his issue was. She got her laptop and suit jacket out of the trunk and headed for the door. The same lady that had been smoking outside yesterday was coming out of the building. She held the door for Carla.

Once in Carla stepped to the side and got a good look outside from a window. The woman made some kind of fast exchange and was headed right back into the building before Carla could get to the elevator. Carla had to think fast, so she opened the latch and dropped her briefcase. When the mystery lady returned, she was picking up papers. She seemed startled, but asked if she could help. Carla smiled and said no, because she was trying to put them back in some kind of order. She made a joke about how the day was starting out. She didn't think that the young lady suspected that she saw her at the car.

After Carla got her things together she went up to the office. There was a small group of employees working. After she put her things in the extra office that had been given to her for her use the prior day, she proceeded to the office of the night manager on duty who was expecting her. To her surprise it was the woman she had just encountered outside and in the lobby. They were both surprised when she introduced herself as Carla Blackstone from corporate Human Resources.

She said that she was expecting Carla and suggested that they get coffee. Her name was Julie Wright. They made small talk, but then Carla got back to business. She told Julie that she wanted to meet as many employees as she could before it was time for her training course at eight. She had a little over a half an hour before she had to set up for class. Carla went around introducing herself and wanted to see if she could get a feel for anyone that may have called her. She had talked to many of the employees over the years and was very happy to make their acquaintance.

The time flew by, and Carla had to prepare for class. While preparing for class, she made a call to the corporate office and left a message since it was still early there, to find out how she could meet with someone in charge of the San Diego office building without asking Paul. She also wanted to know if Erie Technical owned the building, or if the space was leased from another company. Carla wanted to have someone look at the surveillance system in the San Diego office.

• • •

The training class went well. Carla's strategy was to always make sure that her students had retained whatever was taught by testing them with a competitive game at the end of training. She had prizes for those who demonstrated that they had retained the most, or most pertinent information.

After class she called Phyllis Jacobs.

"Thank goodness you called," Phyllis said.

Carla asked her what was so urgent.

She said that her husband had threatened to come to the job to get her and Carla, and a person he thought she was having an affair with at the job.

Carla asked Phyllis who the other person was. Phyllis assured her that she wasn't seeing anyone at Erie Technical.

Carla told Phyllis that she was going to have to give her manager, Pete the details and that she would have to talk to him since she was away.

Pete was already aware of the situation, but needed to know these new, very important details.

Carla thanked her for the alert and got on a conference call with Tom, Pete, and Garrett to update them. Her advice from afar was that they get added security for at least the next week, and everyone agreed. Carla liked to handle everything and was sorry that she couldn't be there to assist more with the strategy.

After they finished, she asked to be transferred to her voice mail. Garrett told her that there would be a message from him. Carla listened to her messages and Garret had made a tentative appointment for her to meet with the facility manager for the San Diego building. The message also said that the company leased the space. Carla took down the number for the contact and called to confirm the meeting with the building manager.

• • •

After lunch with Paul, Carla said that she had to talk to the building manager about renewing the lease. Paul said that he would go with her, but she insisted on going alone and that she would be back for their meeting. Surprisingly, when she met with the building manager, he was very much on top of what was going on in and around the building. He said that he had noticed the young lady in his surveillance tapes and wondered who she was. They had a good meeting. Not a lot of information was shared on Carla's part due to confidentiality, but they felt a sense of trust and that they were both interested in getting to the bottom of what could be a dangerous situation.

• • •

After her meeting with Paul and his manager, she talked with some of the employees and answered a few more HR related questions. Carla loved getting away from the corporate office and meeting with employees in other offices. They always treated her like a celebrity coming from the corporate office, and she loved it.

• • •

She managed to head out the door at about a quarter to five. She rushed back to the hotel, showered, and went downstairs for dinner. She wanted so badly to call Guy, but she wanted him to just show up. She thought maybe she would call him to meet her for a drink after dinner. Midway through her dinner, she was about to make the call when Guy appeared and said, "I guess I didn't impress you enough for you to call me."

Carla smiled and told him that she was about to see if he wanted to meet her for a drink later.

Guy seemed pleased, and believed her. He apparently had started eating at another table and told the waiter he would be moving over to join Carla if it was okay with her.

She said that she would love for him to join her. They talked all during dinner. Then they sat outside of the hotel restaurant on the terrace and had a few drinks. The temperature was about seventy-two degrees. It was a refreshing difference from the fifty degree weather this time of the year back in NC. Carla really enjoyed talking with Guy, but isn't that how it always starts out? Around nine Carla said that she had to turn in, but that she was very happy to have met Guy and that he had made her trip more pleasurable.

"Well, can we just have one dance before you turn in?" Guy asked.

Oh my, she thought to herself, *what it must feel like to be held by Guy*. Well there was only one way to find out. So once again, he had to get her attention because she had gone to la la land. She blushed. As they danced, the aroma from his body was intoxicating.

"You smell good," she said. As they swayed back and forth in the warm breeze, Carla felt very comfortable in his arms. And oh, did he have a set of arms on him.

He was a total gentleman as they danced. Carla was a lady as well. Yes indeed she was a lady as she struggled with the thoughts in her mind that were in opposition with her demeanor. They actually danced through three songs, neither aware when the first two songs ended. They just seemed to both stop dancing after the third song was over. Guy kissed her cheek and said that this wouldn't be the last time that they talked.

Carla thought, *I haven't given you my number and as much as I would like to, I am not going to call you.* I guess he could think that she was going to call him if he so desired. She just didn't have it in her to deal with anymore nonsense at this time in her life. It was nice, but that's all.

CHAPTER 9

The next morning she went to the front desk to check out. Once she completed the process, the clerk gave her an envelope that had been left for her. As she opened it there was a card. In it was a phone card. It said, "Now I know that you wouldn't feel good about using this card to call anyone else." It included Guy's home, cell, and work numbers—two of which she already had. There was another smaller envelope that said, "Don't open until you are on the plane." Carla smiled, and tucked it away. She had too much to do to get excited. She was on her way to the office for the last time before going back home, so she was all about business.

• • •

As she pulled up to the office she checked her voice mail. Then all of a sudden, there was a screeching sound. There were five cars and people jumping out with guns. She heard one shot and ducked down but could see what was going on. They had surrounded the car that she had seen the past two days and had Julie Wright, on the ground. She noticed that one of the men with a gun was the person she had thought was the building manager, but was wearing an official badge.

"What the hell!" Carla stayed in the car, but noticed that Julie Wright, the third shift supervisor, looked right at her as if she had set this all up.

Once all of the commotion was over, she was told by an official that she could get out of the car. The man that she thought was the building manager looked at her and showed his badge. She didn't want to appear to be involved, so she kept walking towards the entrance. She could feel stares piercing holes in her body. She was later notified that there had been an ongoing investigation into a big drug cartel. The meeting that she had with whom she thought was the building manager, unknowingly meant nothing, because he was with the FBI and knew what the plan was going to be the next day. Carla had just driven up at the wrong time.

Apparently, Julie had been a middle person. It reportedly resulted in the state's third largest drug bust ever. They never mentioned Erie Technical in the news, only the building. Thank goodness there were other companies in the building, and the employees knew, per company policy, not to talk to the media on behalf of the company.

After class Carla was ready to head straight for the airport. That was enough drama for one day.

• • •

Once the airplane took off, Carla looked in her briefcase for the envelope that had been left for her by Guy. When she opened it, two coupons fell out. After examining them more closely, one was a roundtrip ticket anywhere and the other was a coupon for a three nights stay with a variety of hotel options. "What the…?"

The note said, "This is yours to do with whatever you choose, but I hope that you will either come back to sunny San Diego, or I will meet you wherever else you would like to go."

So Guy knows what he is doing, Carla thought. How could she not call to thank him for the thought, but she had to mail them back. *I don't know this man*, she thought. His note continued saying that he felt a special bond to her, and that he wondered if she felt it too. "No strings attached, if you choose not to see me again, but please do not mail the tickets back, just enjoy!" As she leaned back to try to take a nap, Carla started to dream about all of the warm places she would like to go.

Carla got back to Charlotte late and went straight to bed. The next morning while in the shower as she swayed to the music on the radio she started to think about Guy. She thought about the way he held her when they had danced only two nights before, and now she was almost three thousand miles away. *He sure felt good and was easy on the eyes*, she thought.

CHAPTER 10

As soon as Carla got into the office she was called into Pete's office. She was updated on the Phyllis Jacobs situation. Then she went back to her office and had answered about twenty messages before the rest of the crew showed up in the Suite. Not many people knew that Carla was back, so she decided to lay low all day. She kept her door partially opened and got a lot of work done for once during normal business hours. As she was leaving she felt like someone was watching her. Carla must have been a little paranoid after all that had gone on in the parking lot in San Diego. After she got in her car and pulled out of the parking lot, she noticed that another car pulled out right behind her and was driving a little too close for comfort. If she found out who this was, she was going to say something to them tomorrow when she got back into the office. Carla slowed down so that the suspicious car would go around her, but it didn't. When she pulled into a gas station, the car sped up and kept going. She couldn't see the license plate, but recognized the car as a dark new model Nissan Altima. She didn't need gas, so she sat there for a few minutes and then pulled off and went home, all the while watching her surroundings to make sure no one was following her. She really needed to stop at the grocery store to pick up a few things but decided against it, since she was beginning to feel tired from the trip and paranoid from what may or may not have just been an incident.

• • •

When she got home, she started to think about Guy again. *My goodness, I have to call him and at least acknowledge and thank him for the thought, but what should I say*, she thought. Was it rude to wait another day to call him? *Oh what the hell, just get it over with*, she thought.

After four rings a strong, sexy voice answered. She was standing, but got weak at the knees, so sat down.

"I was hoping that this was you," Guy said.

"Who," she said.

"Carla Blackstone is the only person that I know of from North Carolina that I have been waiting to call me."

"Caller ID works wonders, doesn't it?"

Guy laughed. "Even before I looked at the number I knew it was your ring."

"I have to hand it to you, you really know how to pour it on, but—"

"Listen Carla, I know that you may not feel comfortable with me giving you those tickets, but don't return them yet. Let's call each other as often as you would like and see what happens. If in six months you don't want to use them to see me, then you can have them as a gift. Is that a fair deal?"

Carla wasn't prepared for this. "You drive a hard bargain. I believe you have negotiated a fair deal Mr. Redding. It will be given serious consideration. I will have my people contact your people within the next six months," Carla said.

"I like it when you talk like that," Guy said extra sexy. They talked for another twenty minutes, and Carla told Guy that he could use the number on his caller ID, since she had never given him her number. After hanging up, Carla thought about why she had met someone on the other side of the country that seemed halfway normal. There was no way she was going to get her hopes up, because he was probably full of it just like the rest of them. Well, at least she wouldn't get caught up this time, since he was so far away. She wasn't going to leave her job, and he seemed to be busy with work and school. So what did she have to lose? It felt good to do a little flirting.

CHAPTER 11

The next day Carla was in the office early as usual, and there waiting for her was Jeffrey Jordan.

"Good morning, Mr. Jordan. How are things?"

Jeffrey said that he was concerned that someone might come to the job looking for him, and thought that she should know. She told him that she would like to bring Tom in on the conversation since it may be a security issue. He reluctantly agreed. Carla called Tom to see if he was in yet. He was only five minutes away, so Jeffrey waited so they could try to come up with a plan to protect him as well as their employees. She strongly suggested to him that he go to the police if he had been threatened. The problem was that he had not been threatened but had been followed on several occasions. He said that he always drove to a public place and once to a police parking lot, and then the person would leave. She asked him for the type of car in case the person came to the job and what he looked like. He said that it was a navy blue Nissan Altima. This response concerned Carla. Could it have been the same car that she believed had followed her? He said that he didn't know what the guy looked like. After Jeffrey left the office Carla told Tom about her encounter with what she believed may have been the same vehicle. On its own, Jeffrey's account without a real threat could have been paranoia and just required awareness, but with Carla's similar encounter there may just be something to his story.

Tom and Carla immediately let Pete and Garrett know what was going on, and they all thought that the additional security they had for Phyllis should be kept a little longer since they had two separate issues.

• • •

Later that afternoon Stacy came to tell Carla that Dale Carson, the man who always thought that he should be promoted or get a salary increase, claimed that his manager had asked him out on a date on numerous occasions and made other comments that were sexual in nature that made him uncomfortable. He had apparently turned her down every time and now believed she was retaliating against him.

"This is just great, isn't it?" Carla said. "What would we do without the drama?" Stacy said that since that was a possible sexual harassment, she knew that she should turn it over to Carla.

• • •

All sexual harassment claims were handled by Carla or Pete. Carla was trying to handle as much as possible, because her manager had been working on the due diligence for a major acquisition. Carla wanted him to spend as much time on it as possible so that the transition would be as smooth as possible. The smoother the transition, the easier it would be on her, because she would be responsible for the details after all of the strategic work was complete. Before doing anything else, Carla started a log. It stated when Dale first contacted HR, when Stacy had notified her, and then she made a call to Dale noting the date and time of her first contact with him. She asked Dale to come down right away and to tell his manager that HR needed to discuss an important matter with him involving his benefits.

As Carla waited for Dale to arrive, she looked in her training log to see if Dale's manager had ever taken the Preventing Sexual Harassment class offered by the company. Thankfully, she had a copy of the attendance rooster with her signature attesting to the fact. At the end of Carla's discussion with Dale, she had him write an account of each incident recalling as much of the who, what, when, where, and how, and if there were any witnesses. After reading the account, there was definitely sexual harassment if the claims were true. Retaliation was unclear. Carla told Dale that this was a confidential situation, but one the company took very seriously. She explained to him that his manager was innocent until proven guilty and the consequences if it were found that he had filed a false claim. Carla told him to go back to work and not to mention anything to his coworkers or manager.

She also told him that she would talk to his manager later that day after she had time to go over the complaint again. Dale's start time the next day wasn't until eleven, so he was told to report to HR first. By then Carla would have time to review the situation with Pete and come up with a plan.

Carla notified Garrett as per policy and told him that she and Pete would keep him abreast of the situation as it progressed in case he had any input. Pete and Carla agreed that they could send the manager to assist a new manager at another office that was about five miles away until the investigation was over.

Carla met with Joyce, Dale's manager, and she explained to her what she was being accused of. To Carla's surprise Joyce didn't seem to take it too seriously. After Carla questioned her, she asked her to write an account of her side of the story. She was told that her rights were being protected as well, but it was prudent for the company to separate the two individuals and because it was a manager/employee situation that it was easier to move her while at the same time conducting needed business at the other site. Carla explained that it was a confidential situation and only the *need to knows* would be involved. Carla told her to come directly to the HR Suite first thing in the morning.

CHAPTER 12

The next morning when Joyce came to Human Resources, Pete contacted Joyce's director and explained that a confidential investigation was taking place and that he would need to make sure that Joyce's duties were handled for a while. To keep the situation discrete, the message to the employees was that Joyce was needed to train a new manager at another facility, which was actually true but otherwise would not have occurred. Timing could not have been better. By the time Dale showed up for work Joyce had been gone for about twenty minutes. Carla updated Dale on as much as she could and sent him to his department.

It was almost lunch time and Carla couldn't wait to go home and get away. She lived twenty minutes away from the job, so that meant that she only had twenty minutes to spend at home, but she did it everyday. In her mind the bottom line was that she was out of the office for an hour everyday. Although she loved her job, it was quite draining. On her drive to or from the office, she would always remember things that she had to do and call her voice mail to remind herself of what she had to do when she got back to the office.

When she got home for lunch she had a message on her answering machine. It was from Guy. He said that he just wanted to say hi and make sure that Carla didn't forget about him. Carla smiled and wanted to call him back, but just didn't have time. She would call him tonight or tomorrow.

• • •

As Carla was parking when she returned to work, she noticed Phyllis in her car with two men. As she was about to head for the building Phyllis called out to her. As Carla was approaching the car, she noticed that one of the other men was Jeffrey Jordan. *It couldn't be*, she thought. As she got closer, she noticed that Phyllis looked terrified. About five feet from the car, Carla stopped, because she knew that something wasn't right. At the same time Tom was just about to enter the building, and Carla thought, *great*, and turned in his direction and called out to him.

At that moment, the other man in the car jumped out with a gun and said, "You better not take another step Ms. Blackstone."

Carla froze.

Tom immediately notified the armed security guard that was just inside the door and dialed 911. As the man with the gun was yelling for Carla to get against the car the guard drew his gun and shouted out, "Don't move." It was too late. The man already had Jeffrey out of the car and the gun to his head. Carla was frozen next to them against the car.

• • •

The police were on the scene in minutes. Carla was visibly shaking but desperately trying to figure out how she was going to make it out of this situation alive. She could see employees all over the building on all floors looking out the windows.

Still holding the gun to Jeffrey's head, the man made Phyllis get out of the car. "Tell them who I am," he shouted, "tell them who I am to you."

"My husband," Phyllis yelled out.

"Louder, so that the whole world can hear before I blow his head off."

Phyllis then screamed. "This is my husband."

"Now tell them who you are pregnant by, and it better be loud."

"Jeffrey Jordan! Jeffrey Jordan!" she screamed as she sobbed historically.

"Too late to cry now," her husband yelled. "And you meddling witch, Ms. Blackstone. What do you have to say now?"

"Mr. Jacobs, I was just doing my job. We had to stop the calls so that Phyllis could do her job. I had no idea what was going on," Carla said. "So what you are saying is that they have done something wrong? Why should you get yourself in trouble because of them? They will have to live with the consequences, and you will have to live with the consequences of what you are going to do today. Please don't hurt anyone. It is not going to solve the problem."

"Shut up with that psychological babble," he shouted, "you should have just stayed out of it. She is my wife, and I should be able to contact her as many times as I wish."

"I don't think that you really want to hurt anyone," Carla said.

"Give me one reason why I should not pull this trigger right now. This man violated my marriage," he shouted.

Suddenly a male voice came over a megaphone. He must have been a hostage negotiator. "Mr. Jacobs, can I call you, Frank?" the voice said. This was a tactic to make a connection by not addressing him as mister, which could imply that he was the person in charge.

"You don't know me, so you can't call me anything," Mr. Jacobs shouted.

Carla noticed a sniper on the roof of the building taking aim. She didn't think that he had been noticed by anyone else.

"I understand that you are angry and hurt right now, but I don't believe that you want to hurt anyone. I know that because we just ran a background report on you, and you have apparently been a good law-abiding citizen up until you were betrayed," the negotiator said.

"I was faithful to her and look at where it got me."

"I am sorry. I am so sorry. I made a mistake," Phyllis pleaded.

Carla thought that she had better not say anything and just let the experts handle the situation at this point. From a distance you could see a helicopter getting closer. It was BMM News.

Frank yelled out, "If they get any closer I am going to shoot somebody."

"Hold on Frank, that's not us," the negotiator yelled, "see the logo, it's the press. Give me a chance to make contact with them to keep their distance."

They went back and forth and on and off for about thirty more minutes, then a woman's voice came over the megaphone, "Son, please don't hurt Phyllis. That is your wife for Christ sake." Phyllis's mother-in-law lived only ten minutes from Erie Technical and had been contacted when they noticed that she was Phyllis's emergency contact in her personnel file.

"Oh mom, you should not have let them bring you here," Frank said in a defeating voice for the first time.

"I wanted to be here son. You know that I have stood by you all of your life, and I will continue to do so, as long as you do not hurt innocent people."

"No one is innocent here, Mom."

"Why do you have that lady, Ms. Blackstone?" she asked.

"She stuck her nose where it shouldn't be."

"Son, do your mother one favor if you have ever loved me. Let her go and then let's talk about this thing. Please, son."

"Mom, go away please."

"I am begging you, Frank." She began to sob. "Please show them that you really don't want to hurt anyone."

"Okay…okay Mom. Blackstone, get the hell out of my face and keep your nose out of other peoples private business in the future."

• • •

Carla slowly stepped away and started to run, not knowing which way to go, to the building or away from it. Before she could figure it out, a police officer had grabbed her. She was taken to a van, given a blanket, something to drink, and then questioned. They wanted to know as much as they could about the three who were remaining. Carla called Pete from her cell phone to provide them information from the employee files of Phyllis and Jeffrey. Pete had them in hand and was already going through them with an official.

"Frank," the negotiator called out again, "do you have a cell phone so that just you and I can talk?"

"Call off your goons," Frank yelled.

"I can't do that Frank," the negotiator said.

Mr. Jacobs had Phyllis get back in the car, but kept the gun steady at Jeffery's temple.

• • •

Pete told Carla that he didn't see anything else in the files that would be helpful. The emergency contact for Phyllis was her mother-n-law, who was already there.

Then Carla remembered that a few years ago Phyllis had come down to HR to ask if epilepsy would be covered under the Americans with Disability Act (ADA). Carla had an idea. She asked the police if it made sense to try to get a message to Phyllis to fake a seizure. Carla never divulged that she thought that Phyllis had epilepsy, but said that she had reason to believe that she may have had a seizure in the past. What if a text message was sent to her in code? At first the officer said that it would be too risky, but then after discussing it with a few others they decided to do so.

A text message was sent to Phyllis that said, "C Sure, See Ur". The negotiator of course, was aware of the plan and spoke in a louder tone, just in case her phone made a loud beep, and a horn was blown a few times when the message was sent

About ten minutes later, which seemed much longer, Frank's attention was averted to the car where his wife appeared to be having convulsions. He called out to her, but she didn't answer. He kept screaming her name. He kept Jeffrey close to him at all times, and they both leaned over, looking in the car window.

Finally, Frank called out to the police, "Get a medic; my wife is having an epileptic seizure." There was an ambulance available, but Frank said no ambulance.

So a plain-clothed police officer (that had been staged inside an ambulance), with medic experience posed as a medic and ran over with a bag. He checked her pulse and heart, and whispered to her to keep up the act. He said that she needed to be rushed to the hospital right away. He asked if he could move her now or he wasn't going to be responsible for what happens to her. "Her heart rate is abnormal and her blood pressure is elevated. I am afraid that she may have a stroke if I don't get her to a hospital right away." Frank seemed to be concerned. The undercover police officer put an oxygen mask over her nose and mouth and claimed to have given her a shot of something to try to stabilize her. The undercover officer was armed but didn't see an opportunity to do anything but remove Phyllis which was his instruction. Frank never even thought that the medic could have been armed.

Jeffrey opened his mouth for the first time and said, "Please help her."

Frank cocked the gun and said, "If you say another word it will be your last." Frank allowed her to be taken away. He had the person that had destroyed his marriage. He hadn't planned to hurt Phyllis anyway.

After she was put in the ambulance it went around the corner with the police officer so that they could question Phyllis to see if she had any information that could assist in ending the standoff. Phyllis was trembling and really did need some medical assistance, especially since she was pregnant. She said that Frank had a good friend that might be able to talk him out of it. The police department contacted his friend who said that he saw it on the news and was already in route. About two hours had gone by. Frank told Jeffrey if he didn't think that they would shoot him, he would make him get on his knees and beg for his life. Jeffrey remained silent.

• • •

After prepping Frank's friend, the negotiator said, "Frank, your friend R.J. is here and wants to speak to you, is that okay?"

"I don't need this, man! What the hell?"

R.J. got on the megaphone and said, "Man, you really don't want to get yourself killed because of what someone else did. You have too much to live for. You know that I always give it to you straight. Just don't hurt anyone. There should be some leniency for you since Phyllis cheated. This is not you, man. Phyllis admitted before everyone today that she is pregnant by another man. That's enough to drive any man to do something rash. Your mom is here, and I am here, we will both stick this thing out with you."

Frank started to cry, but never took the gun away from Jeffrey's temple.

"Man, just put the gun down so that they don't shoot you. We can figure this thing out."

The negotiator took the megaphone back and said, "It's up to you what happens. If you don't want to listen to me, listen to your mom and friend, you know that they care about you. Believe it or not, I care about you too. Things will be so much easier on you because no one has been hurt. Just put the gun down before someone does get hurt."

"How do I know that you are not going to shoot me?" Frank said.

"If I don't do what I say, there are a whole lot of witnesses, and I don't think that I want to jeopardize my career. No one has to get hurt. Put the gun down. Kick it toward me with your hands up, and I will come get you myself."

"I am not going to do it. I am not going to let my so-called wife and this punk have each other."

The negotiator ignored that statement and continued as if they had made an arrangement. "Jeffrey," the negotiator called out, "when Frank puts his gun down, you are not to move. We will come to get you. Please don't do anything stupid. Do you understand?"

Jeffrey shook his head. He was still afraid to say anything since he was warned the last time. In the next fifteen minutes, the whole ordeal had ended, and the news media was everywhere. Carla was released by the police to go home but was told that she would be contacted soon.

CHAPTER 13

When Carla got home, this was the first time in a long time that she felt all alone. She wished that she had a husband or at least a companion to comfort her. Why hadn't she met someone who would just love her, and who she could love back, without all of life's drama? This week had been too much for her, and she was wondering how she was going to make it. She needed a break. She had a bottle of wine that someone had brought over about a year ago, and she was determined to find it. She needed something to calm her nerves. She found it and had just had a sip when she noticed that she had a ton of messages on her answering machine. There were three messages from her mother, one from her sister, and numerous messages from her four brothers, along with other relatives and friends. Carla typically only visited her family about once a year but was giving it serious consideration.

• • •

She had felt removed from the family when she got pregnant as the result of being raped as a young teenager and was sent away to have the baby. Her family did not believe in abortions and neither did she, but in this case that was what she had wanted. She was sent to live with a relative in Atlanta, had the baby, and came back the following year. She never saw the baby. They immediately took the baby to an adopting couple. The only good thing that came out of the trip to Atlanta was the fact that she received very good counseling. Her counselor made her realize that some things that happen in life just can't be controlled and that she couldn't change the past but she can have an influence on the future. This stuck with Carla in all aspects of her life. No one but her sister and mother knew what really happened. Her brothers never understood why she seemed so distant from everyone else, but she had never forgiven her mother. Carla's mother made her beg her father to let her experience the big city for one year. This was the plan that her mother had come up with to keep the pregnancy away from her father and the rest of their family and friends. Because of the secrets, the perpetrator was never convicted, not even arrested, even though Carla had a good idea who it was.

• • •

Carla decided that she should at least give her mom a call. Her mother could let everyone else know that she was okay. When she got her mom on the phone, her mom just cried and cried and thanked God for answering her prayers. After she finally composed herself, she begged Carla to take some time off and come home for a visit. Carla promised that she would think about it and get back to her. Her mom said that if she didn't hear back from her in two days that she would be in North Carolina by day three.

Carla was definitely human, but on the outside, it seemed that she was immortal and had it all together.

She was a pillar of strength for everyone, but this time she felt that she needed help. She had lost her father who she had been very close to only nine months ago. The Employee Assistance Program (EAP) was just a phone call away. As she searched for the phone number, she thought about calling Guy, but then she thought, *I don't know him that well, and he might as well be on the other side of the world with the distance between them*. She finally called the EAP and was on the phone for about an hour with a counselor. They offered to arrange follow-up sessions. Carla declined but promised to do so if she felt it was needed in a few days. She felt much better after the conversation. She just needed to get a lot of things out that she didn't feel comfortable discussing with anyone she knew.

• • •

There had also been a message from Pete, advising Carla to stay home the next day, and that he would give her a call in the morning. Carla never missed work, but this time she had no problem complying. She needed to decompress and get back to some of the people who had left her messages. Carla turned on BMM News and saw the incident recaptured on TV. It was like she was watching a movie. No wonder she had so many phone calls. She felt like she was in a dream and needed to wake up soon. She even pinched herself just to make sure. She felt the pinch and actually laughed at herself for doing so. *That laugh felt good.* The next thing she knew, the phone was ringing. It startled her. She looked at her clock and it was 1:10 a.m. She must have been asleep on the couch for a couple of hours.

"Hello."

"Carla, I am so sorry for waking you up, but I just heard about what happened while I was watching BMM News," Guy said. "I couldn't believe that it was you and your company. Are you okay, honey?"

He doesn't know me well enough to call me honey, but it felt comforting at that moment Carla thought. "Yes," she said, "just a bit stressed." She explained to him what happened less the private details. He was very compassionate and seemed genuinely concerned. He suggested that she take some time off and spend it with family or friends. "It's funny that you say that, my mom just said the same thing. She even threatened to be here in a few days if I don't get back to her."

"Wow, she got her threat in before me," Guy said, trying to lighten the conversation.

"What do you mean?"

"I was going to offer to come out there, too. I can get away for a long weekend."

"I'll live," Carla said with a smile on her face. "But I do appreciate the offer."

"Carla, I can tell that you are leery of me, and I understand because we just met, but I am not asking to stay with you or anything. I can stay at a hotel and just come by when you want me to, or we can just get you out of the house and do some things that make you happy so that you can relax your mind. The only selfish thing here is that I would like to see you again, but I can wait. You will get no pressure from me. You have enough already. I will check with you tomorrow, but feel free to call me anytime day or night. Again, I apologize for calling so late. I just wanted to know that you were safe and at home."

"I appreciate your call," Carla said. "I guess it's a good thing you called. Now I can get in my bed and get my proper rest."

"Kisses on your cheek," Guy said.

Carla smiled. "Kisses on your cheek, too. Goodnight."

CHAPTER 14

The next morning Carla got up, thinking about two things that she wanted to bring closure to: the sexual harassment case and the termination of the San Diego employee, Julie Wright. She had been waiting for information from the police, regarding Julie, so that her final paycheck, an official termination letter, and other documentation like COBRA (legally required offer to continue medical benefits) could be mailed according to California law. Although one might think the government will be taking care of her medical coverage for a while. She was currently out of jail on bail awaiting trial. Erie Technical had suspended her until everything was in order.

When Carla called in to the office, she found that Stacy was going to handle the termination paperwork for Julie. Stacy also told her that right after all of the commotion was over yesterday, George Jones, the older gentlemen in finance, had fallen down the steps and broken his ankle. He didn't want an ambulance to be called, but had his wife come to get him, and he went to an urgent care facility. She had told him to tell them to code it as worker's compensation, and Stacy had already called in the claim. "He said that he has a cast on his foot and can come back to work after two days with some minor restrictions that we will be able to accommodate." Stacy had everything under control, so Carla asked to be transferred to Pete. Once transferred, Carla thanked Pete for the day off. She really needed it. Carla told him that she felt that she could bring closure to the sexual harassment claim by tomorrow. She needed to talk to Joyce's manager and one other witness. This was probably the easiest case she had ever investigated, because Joyce just didn't seem to have a clue. She acknowledged that she asked Dale on at least three occasions in the past month to go out on a date, and she minimized the fact that she had made a few comments that were sexual in nature. "Can you believe her?" Carla didn't teach the class that she attended, Stacy had taught it, and Carla remembered Stacy telling her that she took it as a joke and that it was apparent to everyone in class that she wasn't taking it seriously.

"We're probably going to have to terminate her. I just feel more comfortable getting the rest of the evidence since there seems to be a couple of witnesses. This is very frustrating because, on a separate note, Dale has used it to claim retaliation. Dale has always been a mediocre employee and at least once a year complains that he should be promoted. He is going to have to be more productive and/or take advantage of the tuition reimbursement program to get some additional skills. I don't think that we need to be too concerned here. We have paperwork to back us up. We have also acted accordingly. As soon as we found out about it, we acted, by contacting the victim right away and then separating them." Pete reminded Carla to have everything in writing, and that he felt comfortable with where this seemed to be leading.

• • •

Carla wasn't much for telephone conversations. As much as she appreciated all of the calls, it would probably take a couple of weeks to respond to all of them. She dreaded having to explain repeatedly how she felt. Carla was considering going home to spend some time with her family. She had not been home to visit her family since her dad died almost nine months ago. Although it was her policy to stay away from the north during the winter months she was considering making an exception. From home, Carla scheduled meetings with Joyce's manager and one other potential witness first thing the next morning. By noon Carla took a long hot bath. She believed in exercising and staying physically fit, so she worked out three days a week doing aerobic boxing with other women in the neighborhood.

Carla truly believed that this was what kept her sane. She could release all of her stress with a punch, kick, or yoga technique used at the end of each class. But she also did not believe in denying herself of food that gave her pleasure.

She loved Dunkin Donuts. As a matter of fact once a week on Saturday, she and an exercise classmate would go to Dunkin Donuts and have the number one, a medium coffee and two-donut-special. Carla looked forward to this once-a-week tradition. Nevertheless, she wanted donuts today, Thursday, and she decided to step out to get them. When she got back home there was another message from her mom. She said that she had called the job, and Carla wasn't there and was concerned that she wasn't home. She wanted Carla to call her back as soon as she got the message. So Carla called her back before she sat down to enjoy her donuts. She would make her own coffee today. Last Christmas someone had given her a gift basket from Starbucks Coffee. Carla told her mom that she would be there soon, within the next few weeks. She would check her schedule when she got to work tomorrow and call her back.

CHAPTER 15

The next day when Carla got into the office, the whole group was there early to wish her well. They chatted about things other than work or what had happened earlier in the week before the official start time. Pete let them know that there would be an HR meeting in the afternoon, and everyone should be prepared to update the group regarding their prospective areas.

• • •

Carla met with Joyce's manager. It was discovered that an employee had complained to him that Joyce had made sexually explicit comments about her breast and before he had a chance to bring it up to her, the next day he witnessed her tell a joke that was sexual in nature. He said that he interrupted the conversation and took her in his office and told her about the complaint that was made a day earlier and that he was verbally warning her that if she did anything else like this that he would have to write her up. He had logged the actual date of the conversation in his office.

Carla had him write a statement that included both occurrences. He wrote the statement right then and there, except for the date, which he had to verify after going back to his office. Carla explained to him that this situation was confidential and that he should not discuss it with anyone else. She told him that, most likely, he would need to think about with whom or how he was going to replace her.

Carla had about fifteen minutes before it was time to meet with the last witness, so she checked her e-mails and voice mails. She felt so good about the many thoughts of concern for her. She actually closed her door and cried. *Good tears*. When she opened her door she had her game face on again.

When dealing with business, Carla always had on her game face and every game was like the Super Bowl. After getting a statement from the last witness, it was beyond a reasonable doubt that Joyce had harassed employees and was creating a hostile work environment. She had been warned, she had been trained, she had been told no by her employee but continued to ask him out on dates, and she was a person of authority in the company. She only had three years' tenure with the company, so there weren't multiple years of good service without incidence. She had to be terminated and as soon as possible. Since North Carolina wasn't a state that required a paycheck upon termination, it would be done today. There was no need to have Payroll rush to cut a manual check. Everyone felt okay with this termination. She terminated herself.

• • •

This was the first day in almost a year that Carla didn't leave the office to go home for lunch. There was a deli next door, and Stacy was on her way out. Carla was avoiding being questioned by everyone so she asked Stacy if she would grab her something. Stacy was shocked, because everyone knew that Carla went home every day. While Carla was in her office someone slid an envelope under her door. Obviously, the deliverer thought that she was out to lunch as always. It was a *Thinking about you* card. It was nice and thoughtful, but the wording was for someone that you were having a relationship with. It wasn't signed, and it was too late to try to see who had left it. *Well, maybe someone has a little crush on me*, she thought. She put it in her purse, since it wasn't appropriate to display it on her desk. Carla was preparing for the HR meeting in a half an hour when a strong knock came on the door.

It was the president of the company, Mr. Bradley, and Pete. Mr. Bradley said that he was familiar with Carla's commitment to the company and apologized for what she had gone through earlier in the week. To show his appreciation, he said that he had a bonus for her. It was two additional weeks of vacation, but that it was conditional. He laughed and said that in order to receive the additional two weeks vacation, she had to take the vacation beginning next week and that he didn't know how, but Erie Technical would just have to survive without one of its most loyal employees.

"No excuses, Carla, you deserve it and more importantly you need it," Pete chimed in.

Carla thanked them both and said that she had some things to finalize and that she would do just that. Mr. Bradley actually came over and embraced Carla and held on for a while. He told her that she was a very brave young lady. Carla had tears pressing to overflow, but she held them back with all of her might. She had to keep up her image.

• • •

The HR staff was filing into the conference room and wondering why Mr. Bradley had been in Carla's office. As usual they went around the room discussing various topics. The group was commended on conducting the recent Violence in the Workplace classes. It was believed that it assisted in no one getting hurt during the hostage incident. Apparently, all of the managers ensured that their groups were accounted for and knew what to do if the situation changed. The phones had been switched over to an answering service during the incident. The Benefits Specialist noted that all of the vendor contracts had been signed and that due to the ever changing cost of benefits, they had been redesigned so that both the company and the employees would be able to afford them. The Recruiter discussed his struggles in trying to fill the most difficult, open requisitions. He also discussed hosting a job fair soon. The Generalists talked about processes and procedures to be in compliance with the Sarbanes Oxley Act (SOX), some of the new state requirements in various other states where they had employees, most namely California. The Generalists were also auditing job descriptions and compensation plans. The HR associate and assistant gave an update on their projects as well. It was announced that Carla would be taking a vacation, and there was a discussion about who would do what in her absence. Everyone seemed to be happy that she was taking vacation. Carla didn't know if that was good or bad. The afternoon went by pretty fast, and it was agreed upon that Carla would come in on Monday to finish up a few details and begin her much needed vacation on Tuesday. Carla decided that she would call her mother and let her know that she would be there next week. She didn't want her mother to fulfill her threat to get on a plane and come to North Carolina.

• • •

Carla always cleaned her apartment on Friday evenings. She started out doing this so that she didn't think about the fact that she had no one to spend time with. Somehow Friday nights just seemed like the time that couples should spend time together after a long work week. She would dust, change the linen, disinfect, and vacuum. She loved having her apartment squeaky clean and smelling nice. She would turn up the music and occasionally have a glass of wine. This was her Friday night date, and after a while she had come to look forward to it. This week it seemed to ease her tensions as well.

She finished cleaning and took a long bath. She could always get her thoughts together when she was totally relaxed. One thing that she knew was that she wouldn't spend the entire vacation in her hometown. Once in the tub with all the lights out except the scented candles, she started to think about Guy and the tickets she had. Why couldn't she just go somewhere warm after a few days in her hometown, and he could join her, if he wanted, in a separate room of course? He probably would understand her wanting to go so soon, but doubted if he would be able get away because of school, so maybe that was a good thing. She also concluded that she would call him later to see if he would answer on a Friday night. She had plenty of time, because it was still early on the west coast. One thing that she was sure of was that a man like Guy could have almost any woman of his choice. She started to get anxious about going someplace warm, so she cut her bath a little short and got on the internet to look for possibilities. Before she knew it, it was after midnight. He would never suspect that she would call this late, so she did.

"Good evening Ms. Blackstone, or should I say good morning?" Guy answered.

"Yes it is a good morning."

"This is a pleasant surprise," Guy said. "What are you doing up so late?"

"I actually stay up late on Friday's since it is the only day of the week that I can do so," Carla explained.

"What about Saturdays?" Guy said.

"Well, I can't keep late hours on Saturdays or I wouldn't be able to get up for the church service on Sunday," Carla replied.

"So you are a church-going woman?"

"If that is what you would prefer to call me."

What he didn't know was that Carla felt that she had a very close spiritual relationship with her first love, God. He was definitely the first love in her life. In fact, she hardly did anything in her life without a prayer for consultation. She didn't necessarily agree with the tactics of the bible-toting, sidewalk-preaching Christians. She believed in letting actions speak for themselves. She never wanted to discourage a nonbeliever. They loved to point out the human faults of those who claimed to be almighty Christians. She definitely had human faults, but did try to do what was right.

"So have you decided to take a vacation or take me up on my offer to visit," Guy asked?

"Well, as a matter of fact, I am going to visit my family up north on Tuesday. I am not sure how long I will stay. I was thinking about four days there and then vacation some place warm, like Jamaica for maybe four or five days."

"Wow, that's a change since we last talked."

"Well, since we last talked I was awarded two weeks of additional vacation as a bonus."

"If you decide to go to Jamaica, let me know as soon as you can. It will be tough, but I might be able to work something out."

"So, why aren't you out on a Friday night, Guy?"

"Out like where?"

"Like a nightclub."

"Well, I don't frequent nightclubs too often on Friday nights."

"So do you reserve Saturday nights for your party going?"

"I don't recall making a claim to you that I hung out. I too, like you, have to go to bed early so that I can make the morning church service."

Yeah right, this man will say anything he thinks I want to hear, Carla thought. They talked a little longer and said their goodnights.

CHAPTER 16

First thing Saturday morning, Carla got online and made reservations so that she wouldn't change her mind. She was going to Jamaica next Saturday morning and returning on the following Wednesday night. She went to her exercise class, ran some errands, and before she knew it, it was late. She prepared her clothes for church and caught a good boxing match on HBO.

• • •

Sunday rolled around. Since church started at seven, it was over by eight-fifteen. The sermon was *How to pray properly*, from Matthew 6: 5-13. The points were: 1) avoid public performance 2) present private petitions 3) avoid programmed phrases – a) the Lord's Prayer is a guide or example of how to pray, and how the Lord is not impressed that we can recite this example without thought or purpose.

When Carla got home she cooked while watching one of her favorite shows, Meet the Press. She thought that she had better pack for her trip home on Tuesday since she had to go in to work the next day. She rushed around and had almost everything packed by kickoff time for the first football game of the day. She wasn't sure which teams would be playing in the first game, but it really didn't matter. The second game was the Baltimore Ravens versus the Pittsburgh Steelers. After the second game, she would switch over to ESPN for the late game and call it a night. For the most part, Sunday was Carla's most relaxing day, and she had orchestrated it to be so. She typically did all of her errands and running around on Saturdays, and no matter how much she loved her work she hated Monday mornings, so it took all day Sunday to relax her mind to prepare for another week. She rarely talked to anyone on the phone unless it was her mother or a once-in-a-blue-moon call from a high school or college buddy.

• • •

As usual, who knew what happened to the weekend. Monday mornings just seem to show up unannounced. Carla was met at the door by Pat. Pat said, "I am sorry that I missed you last week, but I guess you got my card. I slid it under your door while you were out at lunch."

"That was from you?"

"Yes."

"Why didn't you sign it?"

"I didn't? I am sorry. I must be losing my mind."

"I understand. I know that you have a lot on your mind and with what is going on at home. Have things gotten any better? You two seemed to be getting along well when we were at dinner last month," Carla said.

"It has gotten worse."

"I am sorry," Carla said. Carla didn't care to know anymore, she just wanted to show her concern and move on, so she said, "I am going to be on vacation after today for two weeks."

"I heard, that's why I wanted to stop by to see you before you left."

"Well thanks. I had better get busy so that I can get out of here at a reasonable time today."

"Okay, I will talk to you later. Enjoy your vacation."

Carla didn't take lunch again and actually felt comfortable preparing to leave at a decent hour. As she was leaving the HR Suite, Pat called out and said, "I think that I am going your way. So when are you actually leaving town?"

"Tomorrow," Carla replied.

"Well, I guess now is as good a time as any to tell you."

"No bad news, I hope," Carla said with a half smile.

"I hope not," Pat replied. "Please don't be offended, but I am only doing this because it is after hours, and you are going to be gone for a while."

"This isn't sounding good, Pat."

"I just need to get it out in the open. You know that person that I told you that I had strong feelings for? Well, that person is you."

Carla's eyes became wide. "You're kidding, right?"

"I wish I were."

"You have really caught me by surprise, and this is just too much for me right now. I will talk to you when I get back." Instead of taking off her jacket and placing things in her car strategically as she normally did, she just got in the driver seat with everything in hand. She wanted to escape as fast as she could. As she was driving away she thought, *does she think that I'm gay*? *What did I do to make this happen*? She really did need this break.

CHAPTER 17

Carla got a good night's rest and was on the road by six in the morning. She had already stopped at Dunkin Donuts and had her coffee and two donuts. It was a nine-hour drive so Carla stopped at three hour intervals for a restroom break and to stretch. She really needed to be with her family to take her mind off everything happening in HR. As always, when she was completely alone and confined to a car for a long time, she started to think. She thought about how to respond to Pat when she got back without hurting her feelings. She really liked Pat, but knew that she was going to feel uncomfortable after receiving such shocking news yesterday. She also liked Le'ann or what she knew of her, and to think that she was the reason that they were having problems. How could this have happened?

After this thought left her, the one that came on every trip entered her mind. Why couldn't she find a good man that would first be her friend, come to love her, and then get married and have a baby? She had been successful in her career so far, but just didn't seem to attract the right guys, and now she had attracted a woman and a guy on the other side of the country. It was going from bad to worse. It made Carla sad even though in public you would have thought that she was totally content being alone. Now she really did enjoy spending time alone, probably more than most, but wanted to have a male companion to visit, talk to, or go out with on occasion. She could do without the marriage and babies, if she could just find a man who wanted to be serious with her.

Thinking and listening to music really made the time go by fast. When she was about an hour from her final destination she called her mother. According to schedule, Carla pulled up in her mother's driveway in the late afternoon. After Carla carried her luggage in, and all the hugs and kisses ceased, she sat down with her mom and enjoyed the best spaghetti and antipasto salad ever. It really hit the spot. By evening her brothers and sister, along with nieces and nephews were all at Mom's house. It felt so good. Everyone seemed to be thankful that Carla was alive and well after the hostage incident. She hadn't realized just how much the ordeal had affected her family.

• • •

Guy called Carla on her cell phone late that evening. He received her e-mail about her arrangements and had arranged his schedule so that he could meet her in sunny Jamaica. This news made Carla both excited and nervous. Nevertheless, she would ponder those thoughts later.

• • •

The next evening the whole family came over again, and they all played cards, listened to music, and sang all of the oldies, but goodies. Then they ate like it was Thanksgiving or Christmas! It was just good old family fun that Carla had apparently forgot about but cherished so much.

A few of her high school buddies stopped by too. Carla had graduated with a class of very good people. The kind of people who were really cool and just good within. Some of the guys were the type that Carla wanted to meet in Charlotte. Even though she loved her high school guy buddies, and some of them were really cute, she couldn't see herself in a relationship with any of them. They were her *buddies* and she would never change that. They were like family brothers, and the girls were like sisters. Carla had really made a mistake in her planning and should have scheduled more time with her family. The visit was much too short.

Carla's stay at home was very busy, but fulfilling. She ran so many errands with her mother until she really did need a vacation. Friday morning she was headed back home, so that she could catch her flight out to Jamaica the next morning. As she was driving home she felt both guilty and stressed. She regretted spending such a short time with her family and here she was, supposed to be on vacation to relax, yet she was rushing down the highway to catch a plane the very next day. *She had to find a way to relax before she went back to work*, she thought.

• • •

Driving back home was just a re-run of her drive up. The only difference was that now she had the guilt of not spending more time there. The good news was that she had really enjoyed it and had another great memory stored in her mind's treasure chest, book of life. This would be a very good chapter. She occasionally got lost in the music without any thoughts. As she was lost in the music, she heard a sound that didn't seem to be coming from the CD player. When she looked into the rearview mirror, it was the darn state police flashing its lights. She immediately looked down to see how fast she was going. She was only five miles over the limit and couldn't believe that she was being stopped. *You have got to be kidding me*, she thought shaking her head. *Why is this happening to me*? As she pulled over, she got really nervous. She had never been stopped before. Although she was lost in the music, she was aware that several cars had been passing her at much higher speeds. She wanted to bring that up, but remembered that she had heard to always be nice to officers.

The officer had been in his car for what seemed like an eternity before he got out of his car and motioned for her to roll down the window. "License and registration, Michelle," the officer said.

Carla looked up. Only two people called her by her middle name. It was Robert Burton, one of her high school buddies that she hadn't seen in about five years. "Oh my goodness!" She wanted to get out and hug his neck. They had kept in touch and talked on the phone about three or four times a year, but always seemed to miss each other when she went home.

"Don't worry, I am not going to give you a ticket, so take that silly look off your face. You don't need any more drama in your life from what I hear." He ended up leading her to a Dunkin Donuts, and they had free coffee and donuts. This set Carla back an hour, but how wonderful it was to see Robert! Robert really looked good in his uniform and was just as silly and animated as he always was. He told her that he had been on a *stakeout* for her. Another buddy that had stopped by Carla's mother's house had told him that she would be headed back this morning. He had gotten a description of her car, and had timed it perfectly.

CHAPTER 18

The next morning, the airport shuttle showed up as scheduled, and Carla was at the door when it arrived. On the plane to Jamaica, the airline served a variety of island drinks. It was wonderfully relaxing and even made Carla start to imagine the sand, water, and warmth of the sun on her skin. Carla kept having mixed emotions. It would be good to spend some time with a male companion and not be completely alone, but he might also prevent her from getting the much needed rest that she so longed for. What had she gotten herself into? Then her next thought was, *Why not just have fun with him, just don't allow myself to get emotionally or physically involved with him.* As the internal debate continued, the airline attendant announced over the loud speaker that they were preparing to land. Now all Carla could think of was the sun, water, and sand.

The travel package came with round trip transportation between the airport and hotel resort. After she exited the plane and proceeded through the airport there was a young guy with a sign displaying, *Carla Blackstone.* This was Carla's first trip to Jamaica, and she was surprised to see that they were traveling on so many dirt roads. She had only imagined beautiful beaches and luxury hotels. When they finally arrived at the hotel resort, the luxury hotel part was true. The hotel was magnificent. Carla thought that she was dreaming. There were palm trees and the intoxicating aroma of beautiful exotic floral arrangements everywhere. Carla checked in and headed to her room. Once in the room there was an arrangement of flowers with a note. They of course were not from the hotel, but Mr. Romantic himself, Guy.

The note said, "Welcome to Jamaica, when you decide that you would like to have company give me a call in room 914 or you could meet me for dinner at 7:00 p.m. tonight at The Oasis." It made her feel good that he had not booked a room on the same floor. It was about one in the afternoon and all she wanted to do was get something to eat and take a walk in the sand. After she slipped into a comfortable, yet sexy, sundress she headed downstairs to find something to eat. Carla found a place to eat on the hotel property with tables outside facing the beach. As she sat down, she all of a sudden felt a sense of peace that she hadn't felt since she could remember.

The temperature was about eighty-four degrees with a light breeze that flowed gently through her hair. The air seemed so fresh. Why couldn't she just stay in this moment forever? While in deep thought, she was startled by the waiter when he placed a drink in front of her. *Wow!* she thought, is this real, or am I *day dreaming?* While she thought no one was looking, she pinched her arm to make sure that she was really there. Then she laughed out loud and a familiar voice said, "Is that a normal practice to pinch yourself for amusement?" When Carla looked up, it was Guy, and what a gorgeous guy he was.

Carla rose from her seat and gave him a hug before she even recognized what she had done. Then she felt a little embarrassed to seem so happy to see him. Her reaction had taken her totally by surprise. He remained standing and said that he was not following her and had wanted her to see him whenever she was ready or later in the evening, as he suggested in his note. He hadn't eaten and was planning to eat there, but said that he was just taking a walk. Then the waiter returned and asked if he wasn't satisfied with his table (which had been right next to Carla's), that he could find another table for him. He was busted, but didn't want Carla to feel like she had to invite him to sit with her. Carla insisted and not out of obligation. He actually fit quite perfectly into the day/real dream she was experiencing.

"Well..." Guy said, confusing her. "You didn't answer my question about the pinch and the laugh."

"I had to make sure that this wasn't a dream. I haven't been on vacation in quite a while."

Guy laughed. "You really have to learn how to relax young lady." Before they knew it, two hours had past. It really felt like they had known each other forever. Although Carla was enjoying the conversation, she kept thinking to herself, *How am I going to resist this man*? He had the most beautiful teeth imaginable when he smiled, and he surely needed to keep his body covered. What would she do when he took his shirt off on the beach? His arms and his legs were definitely that of a man who spent time in an athletic club. But she realized that they were on a beach and that there wouldn't be much covering up. She wished that she would have known him for much longer so that she could have sat in his lap, kissed him, and done whatever she wanted to.

Carla thought that she didn't want to see him right away, but was happy that she did. They decided to take a walk down the beach, and it was just like in the movies. Everything was perfect. Guy suggested that they skip dinner and meet for breakfast in the morning and maybe soak in the sun. He didn't want to seem overbearing. It was well into the evening when they went their separate ways. Carla was going to her room to unpack and look at all of the brochures to plan her next few days.

• • •

After putting her things away, taking a shower, and planning activities for the next day, Carla sat on her balcony facing the water while having a luscious fruit salad she had gotten downstairs and began to wonder about Guy. Could he really be as good as he seemed? What if he was a drug dealer? How could he just up and miss class like this? Where did he get the money for this trip? How was he more gorgeous than she had remembered? What had she gotten herself into? Was this all going to become stressful? Tomorrow she was going to question him a little more. As the sun was setting, she abandoned those thoughts and just relaxed in the beauty of the night. When she came in to retire for the night she called Guy's room. He didn't answer, so she left him a message to see what part of her itinerary he wanted to be involved in tomorrow.

Guy had gone downstairs to listen to a band playing reggae music. When he sat down women seemed to flock in his direction. Guy was polite and talked to a group of women for a while and even danced a few times at their requests. Then he excused himself and decided to go back to his room.

CHAPTER 19

The next morning Carla lay in the bed and watched the sun rise. It was breathtaking. She got up and showered, then decided to call Guy since they had not confirmed a time for breakfast. They agreed to meet in the lobby at nine-thirty. Carla had on another sundress, but this time she had her swimsuit underneath, sunglasses in hand, and was ready to bask in the sun right after breakfast. When she got downstairs, she didn't see Guy, so she sat on one of the many lounge chairs. When he got off the elevator she thought, *My goodness, does he look good in everything?* He had on gym shorts and a t-shirt, and as he was approaching, it made her heart beat like a drum.

Carla thought she really needed to get a life if he was affecting her like this. *No hugs today*, Carla thought. She just got up, they greeted each other and walked in the direction of the many restaurants. They decided on the buffet.

Right after they sat down for breakfast, Carla asked, "So how were you able to just miss class and get away at the last moment? Do you have a laptop with you?"

"One question at a time," Guy interrupted. "I have a confession to make."

Oh no, Carla thought, *here it comes*.

"I told you that I was in school, but I didn't tell you what I was doing. I am a college professor. I teach political science."

"But you are so young, aren't you?"

"Yes, I am the youngest on staff. I went to school seven years straight, including some summers, working on both my master's and PhD. I had the opportunity to work alongside the department head. Once I graduated, I had a decent reputation, and they asked me if I wanted the job. So, I really haven't had time to do any partying. I have been a true bookworm. As a matter of fact, this is the first time I have gotten away since I started, that is why it was so easy. I had not used any of my vacation days."

Yeah right, Carla thought. Guy sensed that she was skeptical, so he produced his staff ID. "I am impressed. I won't tell you what was going through my mind. So, I'm sure that you have some hefty school loans."

Guy didn't readily respond, so Carla thanked him again for the trip.

• • •

Carla reminded Guy of her agenda and told him that it would be a pleasure if he joined her. Guy seemed to be delighted, and then they headed for the beach. Later they would go on a late afternoon island tour and then have a late dinner near the karaoke stage.

The island tour was delightful. Carla began to feel like she had known Guy all of her life. Later they ate and laughed and ate and laughed as they watched the other tourists making fools of themselves singing karaoke. Before she knew it, Carla had had one too many island drinks. She was aware enough to be embarrassed and tried to explain that she normally didn't drink, and when she did she had a two drink maximum. Guy helped her to her room and came in to make sure that she was okay. The next thing Carla knew, she was rolling over and noticed that the clock read four-thirty in the morning. Then she noticed that Guy was lying beside her. *Oh my goodness*! She thought. She didn't want it to happen like this.

Guy noticed she was awake. "Don't worry, nothing happened," he said. I just wanted to make sure that you were okay and that you didn't get up and go out streaking or something."

Carla just looked at him.

"I will see you later. I am going to go catch some more Z's."

Carla just said thanks. As soon as he left, she rolled out of bed and went to the bathroom to try to verify that he was telling the truth. She did still have her clothes on, but it was a sundress. After careful inspection she concluded that nothing happened, then-dragged herself back to bed and fell asleep again as soon as her head hit the pillow.

CHAPTER 20

Carla woke up as the sun was rising. Fortunately, she did not have a headache. She and Guy had not planned to have breakfast, so she decided to go down for breakfast early since she was awake. Their scheduled time for rock climbing was nine-thirty and their massages were scheduled for one. She was sitting down having a light breakfast on the terrace of the restaurant with the breakfast buffet before eight. As much as Carla had enjoyed spending time with Guy, she felt good to be in this moment in time alone. Since the restaurant wasn't full, after she had finished eating she just hung out on the terrace taking in the light breeze until eight-thirty. During this moment of peace she had not thought about Guy, Erie Technical, or anything else.

When Carla got back to the room she noticed that the red light on the phone was blinking. Guy had left her a message asking how she was feeling and to say that he would meet her in the lobby at nine-fifteen.

• • •

As Carla was getting off of one elevator, Guy had just got off the other. They looked at each other, laughed, and said good morning. They had fun rock climbing. Since both were athletic and seemed to have the same level of competiveness, they were equally impressed with the other. It had been a perfect idea to have the massages planned after the climb. Once they got back to the hotel it was just about time for the next item on their agenda. They had to arrive for their massage a half an hour early, so they headed straight to the spa. They were sent to the shower room where they showered, got in their slippers and robes, and met in the tranquil room to await their massages. Carla was about to get a drink from the juice bar and since no one else was in the room to disturb at the time, Guy said, "What can I get you, young lady?"

Carla smiled and said, "I will have a pineapple and pomegranate drink, sir." He poured her drink and turned to hand it to her. Then he pulled it back and whispered, "It will cost you two kisses." For the first time they truly looked into the depths of each others eyes.

"That would be a kiss on your nose and kiss on your neck."

Without hesitation, Carla tilted her head, and Guy gently kissed her neck. This caused a knot to form in Carla's stomach. Then he kissed her nose and smiled. He carried their drinks and allowed her to recline first, then he handed her the glass. He settled in the recliner next to her and took a sip of his drink. Carla took a couple of sips and then put the cucumbers that were on ice on the table between them on her eyes, followed by a dampened cool towel. The aroma coming from the candles was that of the ocean and the gentle sounds vibrating from the speakers was the sound of waves gently meeting the seashore. It was so relaxing. Carla was happy that her eyes were covered, because there was this unexplained explosion going on inside her entire body.

• • •

Guy just laid back and occasionally glanced at her. At this moment he wanted to just pick her up, take her to his room, and gently treat her to everything that he had in him. The French doors opened, and a man and woman appeared, announcing their names. Guy got up and waited for Carla to remove the dressings from her eyes, and he held out his hand to assist her in getting up. The gentleman therapist led Carla first, and right behind was the woman and Guy. To Carla's surprise they were led to the same area. "Are we going to be in the same room," she asked.

"Is that a problem," the gentleman asked.

Carla looked at Guy and said, "I am sorry I missed that detail when I made the reservations."

"Would you like us to make other accommodations?" the attendant asked.

"Carla, it's up to you," Guy said. "It is not a problem for me."

Carla didn't want to seem difficult so she said that it was okay.

Thankfully, there were two separated screens, behind which were the towels that they were to use when they removed their robes. The therapists left the room so that they could disrobe. When they came from behind their screens to lie down on the tables there was no doubt that they were aching for one another.

Guy broke the silence as they were gazing at one another. "Ms. Blackstone, I am feeling a little bad that you didn't give me a tip when you allowed me the two kisses for your drink. Can I get that tip really fast, before they come back?"

Carla melted into his arms, and they had a passionate kiss. Carla could feel the bulge that double-knotted her stomach. "We had better get in our positions before we are caught not following the rules." Then there was a knock on the door. They both jumped on their perspective tables like little children.

Over the next hour, unbeknownst to either, Guy imagined that his therapist was Carla, and Carla imagined the huge hands of her therapist were Guy's. Afterward they took showers again. Carla had a cold shower because she needed to cool down before she met Guy in the waiting area. Because they had come straight there from rock climbing she didn't have clean clothes to change into so she peeked out and asked an attendant if there was a t-shirt or something that she could buy. She would just use the towel to cover her bottom and go straight to the room. It was a resort after all. When she was finally ready, Guy was standing there in the same attire. This impressed Carla. She figured that a man would have just put the same clothes on. They laughed after noticing that they were thinking the same thing. As they were heading to the elevators, it was discovered that the woman had given Guy his t-shirt and Carla had paid for hers. It was just after two-thirty and they decided to meet up again at around five.

• • •

They took naps and were refreshed when they met up in the evening. During dinner they enjoyed each others conversations as usual but with an elevated attraction. Later they relaxed on the beach for about an hour without a lot of conversation, just watching others and taking in the beauty of nature. Then Guy broke the silence and suggested that they get in the water. They splashed around, and Guy was an excellent swimmer. Carla went in the water up to her breast level. Once when Guy came from under the water, he grabbed Carla at the hips. When he came to a full stance they naturally embraced. Then he went back under and came between Carla's legs. She was on his broad shoulders before she could scream. She held on to him around his head. Finally he bent down to his knees, and she was able to dismount.

Then they walked along the edge of the beach for a while. When they returned to their lounge chairs, Guy noticed that the nearby hammock had been abandoned. He checked with the beach attendant and reserved the hammock while he checked with Carla to see if it was okay with her. Carla agreed. Guy got in first and Carla rolled perfectly into his outstretched arm. They lay silently for some time, and then Guy kissed her forehead and said, "You know you fit in my arm just like a glove. It feels so natural. Does it feel that way to you?"

Carla responded with an unexpected peck on his lips, and said, "I feel it too sweetie" These were the moments when she wished that time would stand still for just a little while longer. Finally Carla said, "Are we going to dance the night away since we haven't danced since the night in San Diego on the restaurant terrace. You remember that don't you?" She didn't want to put herself in a compromising position by being alone with him.

"The dance on the terrace is where you first made me weak in the knees. Whatever you want to do is fine with me, but that sounds like a plan." They retreated to their rooms, and Guy asked if he could come by her room to pick her up properly since they were going on a date.

Carla agreed. Even though Carla didn't want to send the wrong message, she felt sexy, and she decided that she would look sexy. She quickly showered again for the third time that day so that she would be fresh and put on the sexist outfit that she had brought with her.

• • •

Of course Guy had freshened up as well. When he showed up he had on dress shorts, sandals, and a short-sleeved button down shirt. They admired each other until Guy handed her a flower from behind his back. "So, are you ready?"

"Yes, thank you for the lovely flower," Carla said. "I think I'll take it with us." She broke the stem and put it behind her ear. Guy put out his arm, and Carla put her hand on his inner elbow, and they went to the lounge where the guests were already dancing traditional Jamaican dances and seemed to be having a good time. After two hours of dancing, they went for a walk. Later they sat at one of the tables in the huge indoor/outdoor lobby and played checkers. It was apparent that they were trying to do anything except end the night.

"Carla, if I promise you that I will be a gentlemen will you allow me to just lay with you tonight?" Even though Carla wanted him really bad, she was firm in that nothing was going to happen, and she didn't want to mislead him. She didn't want to put a damper in the mood, but made sure that she was clear with him that nothing sexual would occur, but that she was tired and would like to spend more time with him.

They headed for her room and decided to sit on the balcony. Guy told Carla to sit on his lap. She did. They talked and kissed and Carla fell asleep in his lap. He just held her for a while and then got up with her in his arms and woke her up as he sat her on the bed. Carla went to the bathroom and changed into shorts and a t-shirt. Now she didn't want to look sexy. Guy took off his shorts and shirt and laid them neatly on the chair. Both of them were asleep in no time.

• • •

The next morning Guy kissed Carla and said that he had better go shower and get his things ready for checkout. They were going to leave the resort at the same time, but his flight left an hour before hers.

They checked out of the hotel, met for lunch at noon, and were en route to the airport by one. They hugged and kissed a long time before Guy departed.

They promised each other that they would stay in touch.

Carla got back to North Carolina about eight. When she got back to her apartment, she dropped her bags at the door, got her mail, and headed straight to bed.

Carla had a few more days to relax before she had to go back to work so she spent a lot of time reminiscing about the wonderful time that she just had with Guy.

CHAPTER 21

Before she knew it, Monday had rolled around, and it was time to return to work. Monday was a good day. She was updated on everything and was able to leave the office at five. Pat caught up to her in the parking lot; she had totally forgotten about their conversation before she left.

"Please forgive me and don't respond to what I said to you before you left," Pat said. "I would prefer for us to act as if I said nothing and continue the way we were. I know that I made you feel uncomfortable and I didn't mean to do that." Carla was relieved.

• • •

On Tuesday, Carla received a call from a male employee, Phil, who had been with the company for ten years. It was a known fact that he was a very committed employee and never missed work. He spoke to her in passing and seemed to always be having a good day. Carla didn't really know him, but felt like she did, because he was one of the few employees that came in about thirty to forty minutes before his shift, unlike most that rolled in about five minutes before start time. At times they would cross paths getting coffee in the cafeteria. The moment he said, "Ms. Blackstone," she could tell that something was different in his voice. He proceeded to tell her that he had tried to reach his manager this morning to tell him that he wouldn't be in today and, now he felt obligated to let someone know that he wouldn't be in today or any other day.

Carla thought that it was unlike him not to give proper notice of his intentions to leave the company. Something had to be going on, so she asked him if something was wrong. He paused and then burst out crying hysterically. "Well, I guess it doesn't matter who knows now. My wife left me three days ago, and she's not coming back. We have been married for eighteen years. I can't live without her." He sobbed. "She was my best friend, and she took Spike with her."

"Is that your son?"

"It's our Collie, but he's like a son, we got him four years after we were married. They're all I have. I am just going to end it all tonight"

Carla knew this was serious, but didn't want to put him on hold to close her door, so she decided to do the stress ball trick. Any time that Carla needed to get off the phone with someone she would throw a stress ball into the hall, and someone would either call her or come to her door. This way she could tell the caller that she had another call. This time she needed someone to come to her door.

Sure enough one of her colleagues called her, but when she didn't answer the Recruiter came to her door. Carla signaled for him to come in and gave him a note to close the door and make sure that she wasn't disturbed. The Recruiter stood there, wondering what was wrong. Carla was very confidential and gestured to him as to say thank you so that the Recruiter would just exit. Then she felt more comfortable talking to

Phil, but knew all along that she needed to get him on the phone with a professional through the EAP. She knew that he really didn't want to do anything to himself or he would not have reached out to someone. He needed someone to listen to him, so she did.

"Phil, you have lots of friends here at Erie Technical. You are a valuable and respected employee here."

"Yes, but they think that my life is all fine just like theirs," Phil replied.

"Phil, trust me when I tell you that many employees here have very serious problems, none of us are without them. I want you to promise me that you will at least give me the opportunity to help you before you do something so drastic," Carla said. "You can get through this. I will stay on the phone with you as long as you need me to, and then I want you to think about talking to a professional from our EAP." Carla explained to him that it was free and confidential. She told him that someone would talk to him over the phone, and then they would meet in person for sessions to get him through this. She asked if he had any relatives or anyone that she could call for him.

He said no, that his relatives were out of state, and that he didn't want anyone to know. He said that he had written a letter that would explain everything to his family, including his wife, after it was all over. After he uttered the word "wife" he began to cry again.

Carla's heart was breaking for him, but she was very strong and confident in these types of situations. When she started to feel like she had his confidence she knocked on her wall and Stacy opened her door. This was another HR unwritten policy. She gave Stacy a note to get the EAP on the phone and let them know that she had someone on her line that needed immediate attention. Stacy went to her office and got them on the phone. She came back to Carla's office and showed her a note that they were on standby.

By now, Carla and Phil had been on the line for about forty minutes when Phil agreed to at least talk to someone else. Carla had made him think of things that he still had left to do in life and any other reason she could come up with to make him change his mind. She told him that she would be available for him to call her back after he spoke to a counselor to let her know that he was okay. She gave him her work cell phone number and told him that she would keep it on. She also asked if it would be okay for her to call him back if she did not hear from him. She verified his numbers and then made the three-way call to make sure that they were on the line together and then hung up. After she hung up, she leaned over her desk and put her head in her hands and just sat there for a while. There was a knock on her door, and it was Stacy asking if everything was okay.

Carla got up, thanked Stacy for taking care of the call and asked if anyone had been looking for her. As Carla stepped out the door, she saw a note on her door in the Recruiter's handwriting. It read, *Do Not Disturb*. The HR group was on the ball. They were such a cohesive group that they could anticipate the others needs. It always seemed that everyone knew just what to do to assist one another. What were the chances of this occurring in the workplace?

• • •

On her way home she decided to try to call Phil. She dialed his home first and the phone went to voice mail. She left a message for him to give her a call at his earliest convenience. Then she dialed his cell phone, and he picked up on the third ring. "Phil, this is Carla from work. I was just checking on you."

He said that he had talked to the counselor for about an hour, and that the counselor had made him an appointment with a psychologist in the area for that evening. He had taken a shower and was just arriving and parking at the facility. He told her that he appreciated her taking the time to talk to him earlier. Carla assured him that it was just a part of her job and that things like this happened more that he could probably imagine. She stayed on the phone with him until she heard him talking to a receptionist. He thanked her again and asked who he should contact tomorrow in case he was out again. They agreed that he would leave a message for his manager again, but that he could call her as well in case he needed to be offered another type of leave.

CHAPTER 22

Wednesday in the HR meeting Stacy said that a manager had reported that an employee had been out for three days without calling in, and she wanted to make sure that it was okay to send out the letter that stated that the employee was a *no call, no show* and had voluntarily resigned. This was a typical policy spelled out in most employee handbooks. Using this terminology avoided terminating an employee and lessened the likelihood of paying unemployment insurance. Rose, the HR Assistant smiled. "Even I can answer that one," she said. "It is in the handbook and reviewed on an employee's first day of work during orientation. I will draft the letter right after our meeting." Rose really did know a lot. She was on the receiving end of most of the incoming calls, whether recruiting, benefits, employee relations, or whatever. They all shared information with her, and after a while she became pretty good at both fielding and filtering the calls for the HR staff.

Pete said, "Not so fast, Rose. Stacy, have we made an attempt to contact the employee?"

"I haven't," Stacy replied.

"I understand that this is our policy, but my past experience says let's give this one more day and know that we made some type of effort to reach our employee. There is a chance that something could be very wrong. Let's leave a message today at the home phone and cell if there is one. If we have not heard back by 4:00 p.m., let's try to call the emergency contact. Then tomorrow morning we can try the home again, and if there is no answer or response, let's send the letter overnight mail. This way we can add to the letter that we made several attempts to reach our employee before sending the letter." This was just another reason why Carla didn't mind working for Pete. He really had a heart when it mattered.

• • •

The next day the operator had an urgent message for Stacy. It was the mother of the employee that had been missing for three days. She went to his home and found him dead. Stacy and Carla called the mother together to extend their condolences and take care of some official business. The mother offered that the cause of death was unknown, but there didn't appear to be any foul play. She was the beneficiary on his life insurance as well as his 401k plan. They notified her of the fact and told her that they would need to have her sign some paperwork when she had the opportunity. They asked if they could share the information with employees once arrangements were made. She seemed like a really nice woman and was happy that it was asked of her. She promised to let them know, and she said that she would come into the office to sign the paperwork rather than having it mailed.

Stacy contacted the manager of the deceased employee and offered an HR representative to be present when he broke the news to the employees in his department. The manager seemed pretty broken up when he was given the news, probably because he had come to the wrong conclusion when his employee didn't call or show up. After his department was notified, HR sent out an e-mail notification, noting the funeral arrangements would be shared as soon as they were made available by the family. Everyone in HR was happy that the *no call, no show* letter wasn't sent out. What a difference a day makes.

CHAPTER 23

On Saturday morning Carla got up early and went to Wal-Mart to pick up a few toiletries. While waiting in line Tom's wife tapped her on the shoulder. "Why hello, Ms. Blackstone."

"Hello Carmen, and hello to you Angel." Angel was Tom's baby girl and she looked just like him. It was nice seeing Carmen, because she was always so pleasant. While they were chatting in line, Carla asked, "So how does Angel get along with your dogs?"

"Dogs? We don't have dogs, thank goodness. All we have is a bird, because Angel is terrified of dogs for some reason. I think it stems from an incident that occurred while I was pregnant with her. That's what my mom says anyway."

Carla thought she had heard Tom speak about having dogs. So to be clear she asked, "Didn't you have a dog or two?"

"No, not after Sport died years ago. It was too hard on the kids, so we decided to get the bird!" On the way home, of course Carla stopped at Dunkin Donuts to get her coffee and donuts, but all the while it kept bothering her because she knew that Tom had said that he had a dog.

Other than the morning sermon, Sunday was a blur. The Sermon title that week had been, *How to have an exceptional life*. Philippians 4:4-9. Carla would review it later in the week and practice incorporating it into her lifestyle.

CHAPTER 24

There had been problems with the elevators, and Carla had mentioned it to Tom on several occasions. She noticed that the required yearly inspection had not occurred and that the inspection certificate had expired, since the certification had to be visibly posted in the elevator. Tom always said that he was working on it. Now an employee was stuck in the elevator. Several employees had contacted HR, so Carla and Stacy went to the broken elevator. Tom was there when they arrived and seemed annoyed when they showed up. He said, "Don't say a word, I have it under control."

Carla asked who the employee was, and Tom said, "Why does that matter? Look Carla, this is a safety issue, and I don't need any input." Tom hated seeing

Carla, because he had not made the necessary contact to get the elevator in compliance.

"Can you hear the employee?"

"Yes, she's freaking out, like the damn thing is going to fall. It's not going to fall, we just need to pry the doors open."

"How long has she been in there," Stacy asked.

"I don't have time for this, Stacy. I called the contractor and they have someone on the way. Elevators get stuck all the time. You guys always want to make things bigger than they are. That's probably why she is freaking out. She knows you guys will come to her rescue."

All of a sudden they heard sirens. "What the hell is that?" He looked at Carla and said, "You called the fire department?"

"No," Carla yelled. She was losing her cool. "I have no idea why they are here," Carla growled.

"This is it, this is the last time you broads are going to get in my business," Tom shouted.

"What are you talking about?" Carla asked. She ignored Tom and moved closer to the elevator to tell the employee that she would be out shortly because help had come.

Tom was steaming. He was pacing, and his face was as red as a beet. By now several employees were standing around and were asked to go back to work so that the firefighters could do their jobs. A very good friend to the employee that was stuck in the elevator was permitted to stay. Carla and Tom bumped heads all the time, but it was just business. She was hurt because he was totally out of character. He was tittering on being threatening. Stacy walked away frustrated. Within five minutes the employee was freed. She was shaking and just wanted to go home. The only treatment she accepted was oxygen. She was hyperventilating. She only allowed one person to come near her. Whenever someone else tried to approach her, she would get hysterical. She didn't want anyone touching her. Later they found out why. She had wet her clothes and must have been more embarrassed than shaken. Her friend took her home.

Because the fire department had come out, it was discovered by them that the elevator certification had expired, and Erie Technical received a fine. The notice went to the president's office, and Tom was reprimanded. Carla usually saw Tom daily but hadn't seen him in two days since the incident, so she decided to call him and make a joke on his voice mail about his behavior. He never returned her call, and when she saw him the following day he didn't speak to her. It was apparent that he was avoiding her and the HR Suite in general.

CHAPTER 25

Laptops started to come up missing, and Tom couldn't seem to figure out who was taking them through the security system. On average one would be stolen every week. The president and CFO had been on his back to find out who was doing it, so he finally came to HR to see if they were aware of any situation with employees or contractors that he wasn't. He had reviewed so many surveillance tapes recently he confessed that he could have missed something. Most of the laptops came up missing in the morning, which meant that the crime took place overnight, but some were taken during the lunch hour when hundreds of employees were around. The police had been called each time so that they could file a report with the insurance company. They also thought that by bringing the police in each time that it would deter the perpetrator's behavior, but it didn't. He or she was pretty consistent. Tom had exhausted the ideas that the police had given him as well. Pete, Stacy, Carla, and Tom brainstormed for over an hour and came up with an old-fashioned plan. Tom was going to put three stripped laptops in offices or cubicles. One was put in a closed unlocked office, one in an office with the door cracked, and the other in a cubical with a locking cable attached. In the past some of the cables had been cut. Each of these locations would have a camera located in a plant. They had agreed that Tom would set up late in the day, and because Carla came in so early, that she would remove the cameras in the mornings.

After three days they caught a young woman who had been with the company for about five years. She walked right into one of the traps. No one could believe that it was her. They thought that she was just working long hours. She had been a good employee. In the end, they found out that she had been living out of her car in the parking lot for about a month. She had lost her child to her husband and had to pay child support. She admitted everything. They fired her, but the company decided not to press charges. This was one of those unfortunate situations. They all really felt bad for the employee, but there was no place for someone like that in the workplace. The bottom line was that she allowed her circumstances to turn her into a thief. She had a choice and chose the wrong path. Carla suggested a program that she was aware of that she might be able to utilize until she got back on her feet. The young lady was very embarrassed, but thankful that Erie Technical had decided not to prosecute.

CHAPTER 26

One of the Erie Technical employees, by the name of Nancy, had a missing child. She had only been a few months old when she was taken from her home in broad day light while the babysitter was taking a nap in the next room. The company had offered Nancy an unprecedented leave for as long as she needed. Everyone was supportive and assisted her on weekends handing out flyers and knocking on doors in her neighborhood. Later her child was found dead as the result of a hit and run. Who abducted the child, how she ended up in the road and who hit her had not been solved.

Nancy wasn't married, and there was never a mention of a father. After several months Nancy returned to work. Nancy and Stacy were friends because they knew each other prior to coming to Erie Technical. Stacy, like Carla, was very confidential, but decided to divulge something to Carla to make sure that she wasn't violating any rules or laws. It was apparent that it was causing her much aguish.

Stacy started out by saying that she trusted that Carla would keep it to herself. Carla assured her that as long as it wasn't something that she had to tell by virtue of the law or policy that she would not. Stacy said that Nancy had had an affair with a married man that worked at the company, and he was the father of her son. She said that the police had wanted to question the father, but Nancy had told them that she wasn't sure who the father was. Now Nancy was wondering if the child's father could have had something to do with the abduction and death of her son.

Wow! Carla thought. *This is too much information.* When she thought that she had heard it all, there was always something new. As much as she loved her profession, and there was never a dull moment, she thought that sometimes her mind was on overload and that she might burnout one day.

"Carla, the father is Tom Benson," Stacy said.

Carla was speechless. *How could her friend do this? How could he do this to his family? They seemed so happy.* Of all the people in the world, she would have never suspected Tom. Even though she was just given this unbelievable news, she knew that Tom was not capable of committing such a heinous crime.

CHAPTER 27

Carla was called to Pete's office where he explained that Erie Technical was going to be acquiring a small company of approximately one hundred employees, and he would need her to keep it confidential. They were in the process of doing due diligence, which meant that Carla had a lot of work ahead of her. She wouldn't be able to delegate this to anyone else because it was not public information. She would have to compare policies, benefits, pay, and much more. It also meant a trip to the site, which was located in Las Vegas. She would have to look at how files were set up and see if they were in compliance with federal and state laws. Going there would not be a chore. Carla loved Vegas.

Was it fate or coincidence? Carla was headed to Vegas, which meant there was an opportunity to see Guy again. San Diego was just a short trip away. She had wanted Guy so bad when they were in Jamaica, and she hadn't stopped thinking about it. If she could see him again soon, she had decided that she would give in to his passion. The thought made her start to sweat. *I am too young for a hot flash*, she thought. *What is this man doing to me? What if he doesn't want to see me again since I didn't give in to him in San Diego or Jamaica*, she thought? Later that evening Carla called Guy to tell him that she would be going to Vegas. He seemed genuinely excited and was sure that he could be there for the weekend, but said he would check to see if he could come early on Friday to spend more time with her. Although she wanted to stay in the same room with him she would not. She let him get his own room again. She didn't want to tell him that her company was getting her a suite and that he could stay with her. She still wanted the mystery, even though the mystery was solved in her mind. She hadn't been with a man in over a year, and she really liked Guy. She realized she would not be moving to California, and he was in such a good place professionally that he would not be coming to North Carolina. She thought, *Why not enjoy this moment in time.* This would be the first time that Carla would try a relationship without the emotions that come along with a serious relationship.

Carla told Guy that she would be staying at the Mirage and thought he would get a room there too, but he had gotten a room at the MGM Grand. Carla was so excited about this trip as the days neared. She could barely think about work, but did what was necessary to be prepared to represent Erie Technical as she always did. Four days before the trip, Pete came to her and said that it was decided that Garrett should go instead of her. She didn't understand why the attorney would go to take care of this part of the process, but later found out that he had never been to Vegas and wanted to go for personal reasons. She couldn't let on that she was disappointed; she wanted it to appear that it would have been just another business trip. One thing that Carla knew how to do was be a consummmate professional at all times. She had broken the news to Guy, and he seemed genuinely sad, but said he had gotten a nonrefundable ticket and would have to go without her. Carla felt really bad that she had inconvenienced him. She did not feel comfortable requesting vacation since she had not been back long. Needless to say, things shifted again. Two days before the trip Garrett had some type of family emergency and couldn't go, so it was back on again for Carla. Even though she was happy that things turned out in her favor, she was a tad bit stressed, because she was now not as prepared as she would liked to have been. Her mind had shifted to park, and now she had to put it in gear to get going again. She decided not to tell Guy since he would be there anyway. She was going to plan something to surprise him.

CHAPTER 28

When Carla arrived in Las Vegas, her luggage did not arrive with her. She had learned over the years of traveling, that this was a very real possibility, so she always carried one change of clothes with her in her carry-on so that she had something until her luggage arrived. With the time change, she arrived in Vegas around noon. She made it to her hotel, checked in, and devised a plan by late afternoon. She had a good reason to go to the mall. She would buy a business suit as a standby in case her luggage didn't materialize before morning. On a trip a few years prior, she didn't receive her luggage for three days. Another passenger had mistakenly taken it, dropped it off at his home, and didn't realize that he had the wrong luggage until he started to unpack. Carla's plan was to get a suit, get something to eat, and go back to her room to go over her checklist for the following morning. She planned to call Guy when she got back to the room and make plans to see him sometime the next evening.

• • •

It didn't take her long to find a business suit. Since Carla wasn't big on eating out she thought that it would be safe to choose a recognizable restaurant. She ordered a drink to go with her salad while she waited for her meal. A man with a familiar body walked by, and she couldn't believe it. It was Guy. She almost called him, but began to think, *What if he is here with another woman or something.*

She got tense and watched until he sat down. He sat down across from a well dressed gentlemen. *Maybe he had got one of his buddies to come with him*, Carla thought. She wiped the sweat that had beaded over her brow. When his companion got up and headed towards the men's room, Carla went over to speak to Guy. He was of course shocked and surprised. She explained herself as he walked her back over to her booth. He said that he was with a buddy but could cancel their plans to see her tonight. She told him that she had planned to call him later so that they could meet tomorrow. About that time his buddy was back at their table. Guy gave Carla a hug and told her that he had to get his buddy back to his job.

"He lives here in Vegas?" Carla said.

"Yes," Guy replied. "I will give you a call later to find out about tomorrow."

Carla thought it was strange that he didn't introduce her to his friend, but they seemed to be in a rush to leave.

Then they both did a u-turn at the door and approached Carla's table as her meal was being served. Guy said, "George wanted to meet you." He introduced them, and George seemed to want to know everything about Carla, how they met, how long she would be in town, etc. Guy cut him off and said, "I will tell you all about her, but now you better get back to work before you get fired." George was just about as handsome as Guy, so Carla didn't mind his questions.

As they went into the mall area, Carla could still see them. She noticed that George smacked Guy on the butt, like men do in basketball games. Carla thought that was strange but dismissed it. Then her mind began to wonder. She told the waiter that she would have her meal to go. She finished her drink, left a large tip, and departed. She saw the exit that Guy and George had went out. It was the same area in which she had entered the mall. She stood to the side until she saw them get in the car and pull off. She hurried to her rental car, put on her sunglasses, and attempted to catch up to them where she would not be noticed. She was able to do so and amazingly made each traffic light.

Guy was driving and pulled up to the Mirage. When he let George out, George came around to the driver's side, put his head in the window, and gave Guy a kiss on the lips. Carla could not believe what she had just witnessed. She almost threw up. She sat there for a while with her head in the steering wheel until a hotel bellman walked down the long sidewalk and knocked on the window. He asked if she was okay and said that she would have to move her car. She explained that she was a hotel guest and was feeling sick. She decided to let him park her rental instead of parking it herself. As Carla walked through the casino she was in a daze. She never heard the familiar sounds of an active casino. Somehow she made it to her room. Once she was in the room, she couldn't remember how she got there. Carla sat on the edge of the bed and began to sob. *What had she missed?* Was this what they called, *the down low?* She had been prepared to possibly sleep with this man.

A knock at the door startled Carla. She looked at the clock, and it was 7:35 p.m. She had apparently dosed off. She sprung up without thinking and looked out the peek hole. She didn't see anyone, and had no intentions of opening the door. She thought that if it were the hotel staff they would have said housekeeping or something. Maybe she had been dreaming. Either way, she was glad that she was awake. She needed to look over her material again. *Okay, let's get in gear*, Carla thought. "I need water, coffee, and a shower." She grabbed the ice bucket and opened the door.

Before her was the most beautiful flower arrangement that she had ever seen. She froze in place for a moment before regaining herself. She placed them in the room and proceeded to get ice and water down the hall. There was no question in her mind where they came from, so she didn't look at the card. When she returned to the room, she decided to get right in the shower and try to run her emotions down the drain. She barely turned on the water before she was inside. She couldn't hold it in any longer. She began to cry again and let the water wash away her tears. Carla was a strong believer in mind over matter. If she could trick herself into thinking that she could let everything out this way, she would get out of the shower, dry off, and wipe all this mess away. This was why Carla took long periods of time between dating. It always hurt her to the core. Each time it was the same song replaying, deceit, deceit, deceit! Why couldn't men just be truthful? She could handle the truth. *In this case*, she thought, *the positives were, the sooner she found out the better, and the fact that they didn't live in the same town, so she didn't have to worry about running into Guy anymore.*

When she stepped out of the shower, the aroma from the roses had permeated the whole room. Carla loved flowers, and the smell of roses was like aroma therapy. She never considered throwing them away and had decided how better to find out about the games that men play then to read the card. After reading it she felt stupid and relieved at the same time. She had gotten herself worked up over nothing. The flowers were from the company that she would be visiting the next morning. The note welcomed her to Vegas and gave her directions to the hotel entrance where a car would be waiting in the morning. This felt good. Then there was another knock at the door, and someone announced that her bags had arrived.

Carla opened the door, and there was her luggage. She gave the gentleman a tip and closed the door. *Things are looking up*, she thought. No sooner than she started to look through her bags, then there was another knock at the door. Without thinking, she opened the door.

It was Guy. He had on blue jeans that were made for his body, a cream-colored pullover light knit top—with three buttons at the top that were open, with a black casual blazer. For a moment Carla almost forgot how upset she had been. Because she was still standing there, then he asked, “Are you going to let me stand here all night?”

She told him that she thought that they were going to make arrangements tonight on the phone about tomorrow, all the while knowing that she had no intentions of ever talking to him again.

“I couldn’t wait, so I took my chances and decided to stop by.” From behind his back he produced a beautiful bouquet of flowers. As he handed them to Carla, he leaned over to kiss her. She gently turned her head, and his lips made connections with her cheek. It made Carla cringe. Since he was there, she thought why not just see what she could find out, so she moved aside. As he stepped in, the aroma of his body gently kissed her nose.

“I didn’t tell you why I was at the mall. I was there because my luggage had not come with me when I arrived. I had found something just in case the airline had not located it before this evening. It was just dropped off right before you came, so I still have to unpack and prepare for tomorrow."

Guy noticed the roses that she already had and seemed to be disappointed and commented, "And to think I thought that I was going to impress you. I guess I am a little late."

"Those are from the company that I will be visiting tomorrow," Carla said, wishing that she could take it back. He didn't need to know where she got them. He didn't seem to believe her, and she didn't try to explain anymore. "I thought that you and your friend were going out tonight," Carla said.

"After I dropped George off, all I could think of was you, so I called him and told him that I would get with him tomorrow afternoon while you are working."

Carla thought to herself, *I am sorry you wasted your time.*

Carla started unpacking and casually had conversation. Guy had been sitting down, but got up and came behind her and massaged her shoulders. While it felt good, she cringed again. "So how do you know George," she asked?

"You are acting just like George. He wants to know all about you. Can't I just keep you two separate? I am here to be with you. I will tell you about him another time."

This made Carla so mad, she could no longer keep her cool. "Look, Guy," she said, "I don't know what kind of games you are playing with me, yourself, or with George for that matter, but I am a straight female. I don't do threesomes, or get intimate with men who are intimate with other men." Guy had already removed his hands from her shoulders and was looking at her as if he saw a ghost. "I don't understand you. I better understand men that like men, or women that like other women, but you are confused and very confused if you think that I am going to get involved with someone like you. Does George like men and women too, or just you? I thought that you actually cared about me."

Guy interrupted with a nervous laugh. "Carla, are you accusing me of having a relationship with a man, because I was having lunch with George?"

Before he could continue, Carla chimed in. "Please don't start with that male denial thing. I have been there and done that, and for your information, I know exactly how it works. You say it wasn't me unless you were approached as something was actually happening, and even then, you might deny. I saw George slap your butt when you two were leaving the mall."

"Are you kidding me, Carla? You saw that, and think that I am gay."

"No Guy, I also saw him kiss you right in front of this hotel earlier."

Guy just put his head down, and Carla said, "I think that you should leave now."

As Guy was leaving he said, "I promise that I will explain one day, hopefully soon."

Carla looked up and said, "Lord, you sure do have a sense of humor. I do not know why this has happened, but I am sure that you will let me in on the punch line later." Then she didn't feel as bad. Guy was as guilty as sin and didn't continue to lie. She was now exhausted, so she finished getting her outfit ready for the next day, set the clock, and fell right to sleep.

CHAPTER 29

The next morning Carla woke before the clock alarmed. She hoped that the prior night had been a dream, but she looked up and saw all the flowers. She didn't pinch herself this time because the flowers were evidence that she was in reality. She turned the TV to BMM to see if anything had happened overnight. After the headlines didn't reveal any major changes in the current worldwide madness, she went over her notes one more time, dressed, and headed downstairs for the continental breakfast. The car the company was sending was due in thirty minutes. She selected coffee, an apple danish, and a banana. As she was about to eat, she started to feel sad, and maybe she had forgot something. She had forgotten to say grace. Carla was so thankful for everything, the good and the bad, and never forgot to say grace. She bowed her head, gave thanks for her food, and prayed for the strength to get through the day without tears. She felt much better when she lifted her head. When she finished and headed for the exit of the hotel, she looked around thinking that maybe a celebrity was nearby when she saw an extra nice limo outside. Then the driver asked her if she was Carla Blackstone. *Wow!* Carla thought, trying to mask her excitement when the driver opened the door for her. Once she was in, it dawned on her that it was the company attorney who was supposed to come, and they had probably already made arrangements for him and decided not to cancel them. Nevertheless, she was happy that she could reap the benefits. The driver gave her a welcome package that included goodies and a schedule of her day to review. She was also offered an assortment of drinks and snacks, but declined since she had just had breakfast. Once they got to the office, the driver opened the door and escorted her to the door where the executive assistant, Rachel, to whom she had spoken to before, was there to greet her.

Carla thanked her for the beautiful flowers that had been sent to her. She knew that the assistant would have been the person taking care of something like that. She was then introduced to the company president, who took her around for more introductions of high level executives. For the first time Carla felt this assignment may have been a bit too big for her, and maybe Pete or Garrett should have come. This thought came to mind solely based on the flowers, the limo, the physical elegance of the office and the status of the top management who all seemed to be wearing tailor made clothes. These things never fazed Carla, but in this instance everything was so conspicuous. The office reeked of excess, although exquisite. You would have thought that it was Donald Trump's office. After morning meetings and lunch with the top brass Carla set out to do what she knew. She was given both an office and conference room to go over files, policies, and a whole list of other items. They had everything in order that had been requested in advance. She finished up around four-thirty. There was a scheduled informal dinner planned for six at her hotel. Earlier she was told that the men would wear something akin to khakis and polo shirts. So Carla would dress causal, but just above that. If nothing else, this company knew how to look impressive.

• • •

Although Carla hated business lunches and dinners, this one was surprisingly enjoyable and productive. By seven forty-five, Carla was heading back to her room when she decided to put just one quarter in a slot machine. As she put it in she noticed Guy, but he didn't see her. He was talking to two other guys, and the conversation looked really intense, so she decided to stay a little longer. The cocktail waitress asked if she would like a drink, so she ordered a glass of wine. She was in a perfect spot to spy, *But why am I*, she asked herself? Guy left, but appeared again, moments later, with George. The two gentlemen he had just had a conversation with didn't acknowledge his presence. Carla decided she would exit as soon as she saw an opportunity where Guy would not notice her. Something just wasn't right, and she was not that interested in whatever it was. Back in the room, the situation in the casino bothered her, but she put those thoughts out of her mind, took a shower, and prepared for the next two days ahead of her. She had a lot to do, other than worry about a man who seemed to be involved in some type of shady lifestyle. Good thing she was out of it.

CHAPTER 30

The next day no meetings were held, just a scheduled lunch. Carla read so many documents that she felt her eyes were going to cross. This was a two person job, and she wished that someone else could have come, although Garrett would still have to come out soon. He and the CFO had apparently taken care of most things via e-mail and teleconference over the last few months.

• • •

On Carla's final day in Vegas she finished up right in time for a three o'clock overview meeting. What she had discovered was that the files, processes, and systems were in better order than Erie Technical. They seemed to be in compliance with everything. The reason that they were having financial difficulties and needed buyers was due to excessive spending. The reason everything was so orderly was because they had too many employees and too many outsourced vendors for the Human Resource Department as well as every other department, it seemed. Their salaries were well above local and national benchmarks, as well as their medical plans and executive compensation plans. There would definitely be a problem, trying to figure out how to merge the excessively overcompensated employees into Erie Technical. Because of the downsizing that had occurred a few months earlier, Carla wanted something positive like this to happen so that Erie Technical employees would see that things were on the upside.

After the meeting Carla said her goodbyes and thanked everyone for their hospitality. After she was back at the hotel she changed and decided she would spend the rest of the evening taking advantage of whatever the Mirage had to offer. She decided on the Chinese food restaurant, and the food was fantastic. After dinner she walked through the area where the shops were located. While walking back in the casino area, Carla noticed a sign that a band would be playing.

She decided that she would drop off the small items that she had purchased, get a news update on BMM, pack her things for the next day, and come back down to hear the band.

When Carla came back down to the casino she headed straight to the lounge, and the band was just about to start. It was pretty crowded. The waiter told her that all of the tables had been taken, but that there was a female alone that said she would be happy to have company. Carla decided to sit with her. She introduced herself, and they hit it off right away. They were both in Vegas on business and both leaving the next day. The band was great. At one point when they were singing a slow song Carla thought about Guy. She thought how she had planned on enjoying a show like this with him. That thought went right away when she thought about George. She was happy that she hadn't run into either of them again.

• • •

The next day, Carla took the rental car that she barely used to the airport and boarded her flight. While relaxing on the plane she had made the decision that she was going to spend more time talking to and visiting family and friends. This was going to take effort on her part, but it would be a deterrent from the thought of ever having a meaningful male relationship. She would devise a plan when she got back to Charlotte. Maybe she would call at least one friend and one family member per week. Based on her past record, this would be a valiant effort.

CHAPTER 31

Back in the office the following day, Carla met with Pete and Garrett to give them a copy of her report. She couldn't put her finger on it, but she detected that something wasn't right. Maybe they had decided against the acquisition and were going through the motions with her since she had just worked at compiling all of that information. She would ask Pete what was going on later. When Garrett left the office, Pete kept asking Carla about all of the things that she had been working on and what she felt were the most pressing items. Carla was all too familiar with this line of questioning. It was what typically happened when someone was about to be let go, but that couldn't be. They loved and counted on her. After all she had just returned from a very important assignment. This made her nervous, so she asked Pete if something was wrong. He said, "Yes," as he was getting up to lead her out. He said that he had to dial into a conference call, and they would talk later.

• • •

Carla went into her office and sat at her desk. Then a knock came at her partially opened door, and two tall handsome men were standing there. This was unusual because outside guests had to stop at the security desk, and the guard calls to announce when anyone has a visitor. One of the gentlemen said, "Are you Carla M. Blackstone?"

Carla answered, "Yes," and the other gentlemen said, "You are under arrest for hit and run."

Carla said, "You must have me confused with someone else."

"You have the right to remain silent…"

Carla continued to protest when one of them said, "We have all of the evidence we need Ms. Blackstone. Now get your purse, and let's do this as dignified as possible." Carla said, "Oh, okay, the HR team must be playing a joke on me," so she would go along with the joke. She got her purse and said, "Take me away." As they stepped out of her office there stood Pete, Garrett, and Tom, and they were not smiling. At this point Carla realized that this must not be a joke. She said to Pete, "Please believe me, this is some kind of mistake. I will clear it all up."

Carla was placed into the back of an unmarked police car that was behind the building. They had not handcuffed her. Once Carla was in the car, she said, "I don't understand what is going on."

"Madam, be happy that your employer helped us make arrangements not to make a spectacle of you and to be as discrete as possible," the officer said. With that, she was then handcuffed and they drove off.

A million things went through Carla's mind. She had always been told that if anything like this ever happened to exercise the right to remain silent. *What will my family think? Who am I going to call? I don't have an attorney. Did I hit someone without knowing it?* She decided to do what she has done in the past. She pinched herself, and no, this was not a dream, but it was a nightmare that was very real. When they got to the station, Carla was fingerprinted, and had her mug shot taken.

CHAPTER 32

Carla picked up the phone to make her one phone call. She had decided rather than call her family that she would call her friend Cathy.

Cathy was Carla's best friend, who would come to visit her for the weekend about twice a year and spend one week with Carla each summer. Carla so enjoyed their time together. She would always take off on Thursday and Friday of the week and hang out with Cathy. This way, including the weekend, they would have four full days of activity. It would be the only time Carla would have to force herself to do something other than work. They would go to plays, movies, concerts, and pretty much Carla's once a year visit to a night club. Carla always enjoyed dancing at the night clubs, but just couldn't bring herself to make it a habit. That was why she enjoyed it so much the few times that she went. She would always go as an alias. Most of the time her name would be Charlene, and she would not give out her phone number to those that inquired, with the exception of those that just persisted, and then she would reverse one set of numbers. That way in case she ever saw them again she could say that they took the number down wrong. There would be times that she was interested in some of the guys, but she was always told that a bar was not the place to meet a good guy. Even though she was smart enough to know that there had to be a few good men in nightclubs, she was not willing to try to weed them out, no matter how interesting or how handsome they looked to her. Deep down she wanted a relationship but did everything not to have one.

• • •

"Hey, girl," Cathy said when she realized it was Carla on the other end. Then almost immediately she knew that this was a serious call. Carla explained the short version of the story and that she really needed Cathy to come to Charlotte if she could, that she needed an attorney, and not to contact her family. Carla knew that she could trust Cathy to do whatever she needed. Cathy took notes on all of the important information so that she could get help for Carla.

• • •

Before the end of the day, a lawyer showed up to see Carla. Carla explained everything that she knew about her arrest, which was very limited. No one had borrowed her car, and she had not hit anyone to her knowledge. She explained that the police had told her that they found a very small piece of the blanket that the child was wrapped in lodged in the internal side of the grill of her Mercedes. Her lawyer said they would have a hearing the following morning where bail would be set.

• • •

The following morning Carla's lawyer explained to the judge that Carla was a stellar citizen without any blemishes on her record. She had not run thus far, and the accident had been months prior. Carla had the money for bail and was taken to a car rental agency by her lawyer. Her car had been impounded. She was supposed to be able to retrieve it in 3 days. As she was driving home, her cell phone rang. It was Cathy. Cathy was happy to hear that she was out and said that she would be in town the following day and would be able to stay for five days. Carla was so thankful.

Carla asked her lawyer to contact Erie Technical to request a thirty day leave of absence. The request was made, and the paperwork was to be mailed right away. This way she would have some breathing time to try to make sense of this all.

• • •

It had hit the local news stations that an arrest had been made in the hit and run of the baby after months of investigation. Stacy was with Nancy, the mother of the baby when they found out that it was Carla that had been arrested. Stacy was confused, but felt that there had to be something shady going on. She did not believe for a minute that Carla could have had anything to do with this. It just didn't add up. Tom was the one that had been acting strange lately, so she urged Nancy to come forward and confess that she knew who the father was and tell the authorities who she suspected. Nancy told the authorities that she had an affair with a married man, Tom Benson and suspected he had something to do with the abduction but couldn't prove it. As a result, Carla's lawyer was able to have the body exhumed. An autopsy was completed, and it was found that the child had been suffocated and died before it had been hit by a car. After further investigation it was found that Carla's favorite work colleague was responsible for cheating on his wife, kidnapping and suffocating his child, and placing him on a scarcely traveled road that he knew Carla would be traveling on a late rainy evening after they had worked late. He had apparently had the deceased child in the trunk of his car for two days before he saw the perfect chance to set someone else up. It just so happened Carla gave him the perfect opportunity. She had told Tom that she would be taking the back road to get home that evening because of a traffic accident on the main road.

Tom had gotten a head start and called her on her cell phone, which had distracted her. When he knew she was around the bend he placed the child in the road and stood behind a tree nearby.

• • •

Later Carla was able to recall that conversation. She had been driving in the rain talking to Tom Benson on her cell phone. She remembered hearing a noise and then dogs in the background while talking to Tom. It was all coming back to her. *If I would have only not answered that cell phone I would have been more alert*, Carla kept thinking.

The investigation process was fast and took just over three weeks. DNA evidence of the child was found in the trunk of Tom's car and a team of police recruits went back to search the wooded area near where the child was hit and found a button that turned out to be missing from a windbreaker that Tom had worn that evening. The timeline between the time that he abducted the child and the time that the child was found was not yet discovered. Tom may have had an accomplice keeping the child for a short time. The charges against Carla were dismissed, and she was prepared to go back to work the following week when her leave of absence would be over.

CHAPTER 33

A few weeks after Carla returned to work she happened to be in the lobby when the son of Debra Freeman was standing there again waiting for his mother. Carla smiled at him and extended her hand, asking him if he remembered her from a while back when he was there before. He returned a bright smile and said that he did remember her. At that moment Ms. Freeman got off the elevator and went into a tyrant where everyone around could hear. Carla stepped back. Pete had come out of his office to see what the ruckus was about. Ms. Freeman confronted Pete while pulling her son by the hand. "See I told you she was meddling in my business. He is not her son, he is mine!"

Carla's mind raced back to when her mom had sent her to Atlanta when she was younger. *It couldn't be*, Carla thought.

Pete told Ms. Freeman that she needed to come to his office or leave the building immediately. She decided to leave. As she stormed out, Pete handed her a business card and told her she would have to call him before she returned to work.

Once she was out of the building, Pete alerted the guard not to allow her to re-enter the building, without notification from HR that it was okay for her to return. Pete told Carla to follow him. He seemed very annoyed and told Carla, "You need to let me know what is going on between you and Ms. Freeman."

Carla started to cry, "I promise you that I do not know Ms. Freeman, but I might know what she is talking about." Carla told Pete that she had to have his total confidence. Pete promised, and Carla felt that she could trust him. She told him about being sent away and having a child that was adopted, but that she had no way of knowing if this was the child. His perceived age was right, and it would provide an explanation for Ms. Freeman's behavior.

• • •

Ms. Freeman's son always knew that he was adopted. After he and his mom had been silent in the car for about ten minutes he asked his mom, "Was that my birth mother?" Ms. Freeman began to cry. She pulled over into a shopping center parking lot, and they both cried.

• • •

Ms. Freeman called Pete later and apologized. She said that she wouldn't be in that afternoon, but would explain everything to him in the morning. That evening she and her husband talked to their son, Justin about Carla. Justin assured them that he felt they were his true parents, but that he wanted to meet with his birth mother.

• • •

Carla was pretty distraught. Pete understood and told her to go home for the day. Driving home she knew that she had three options, to talk to her mother, sister, or the aunt who she stayed with when she had gone to Atlanta. She didn't want to bother Cathy again so soon. Once home, she decided to wait until Ms. Freeman came in the following day before jumping to any conclusions. If need be, she had decided that she would call her sister since they had just recently had a good visit when she was home. If she called her aunt first, and her mother found out, it would probably hurt her mother's feelings. She spent most of the evening on the internet trying to search for any clues about the Freemans she could think of, but nothing concrete emerged. Later emotions flooded her mind. She was drowning in thoughts of the tragic incident that occurred years ago. *Did that monster harm any other young girls? What if it really was my son that I saw twice? Would he want to get to know me? What if he doesn't? Will he resent me? What were the employees thinking that witnessed the incident? Why is this happening to me?*

She must have slept for two hours, and then it was time to get up. She put cold compresses on her face to try to sooth her stress and swollen eyes. Somehow she got it together and made it into work at her normal time.

When Ms. Freeman came in the following morning, she was escorted to Pete's office by the guard. Carla made sure that she was in her office with the door shut. Within ten minutes, Pete knocked on her door. He asked her to come into his office and let her know that Ms. Freeman was still there. Carla nervously followed without saying a word.

• • •

Debra Freeman apologized to Carla for the way that she acted towards her the prior day, as well as the other time that Justin came to meet her for lunch. She explained that she knew from the day that she started at Erie Technical two years ago that Carla was the mother of Justin, but had been able to avoid her because she didn't want to lose her son. Carla broke down in tears. It was true. Justin was her son. Debra was able to explain everything. She also shared a copy of the adoption papers with Carla. Pete felt comfortable that the two ladies could talk and that it was too personal for him to stay, so he excused himself. Debra actually came over to console Carla.

• • •

Carla met with Justin and his parents that weekend at their home. The Freemans had done a great job with him and had even explained the circumstances of the adoption. Carla said that she would be available anytime that Justin wanted to see her as long as it was okay with his parents. Carla and Debra became good friends, and Carla decided to wait a while before she shared the news with her family and Cathy.

CHAPTER 34

About three months after Carla had found out about Justin, she received a call from a number that she didn't know. Normally she would have never answered a call from an unknown number. She would wait to listen to the message. This time she just picked up. It was Guy. She started to hang up, but always thought that was a rude thing to do. As soon as he announced himself and pleaded to be heard, she wished that she had not picked up the phone.

"Carla, please just listen to me for two minutes. I know that I am the last person that you expected to hear from."

Carla was silent.

Guy began again, "First, I am not gay or close to it, I have two jobs at certain times, and can explain and show you evidence of everything, if you will just give me the chance. I know that I am asking a lot, but you mean a lot to me and all I want you to know is that my feelings for you were genuine. I am in town."

Carla interrupted, "What do you mean, you are in town?"

"I have been in your area for about a month now," Guy replied.

"I don't understand."

"I don't expect you to. I am just asking you to think about seeing me so that I can explain. I would like to take you to dinner. I don't expect you to answer right now, but think about it, and I will call you back tomorrow," Guy said.

"I really don't know what to say to you, but I have to go," Carla said.

"All right. It was really nice to hear your voice again. I will call you back soon. Goodnight," Guy said.

"Goodnight," Carla said.

• • •

A week later Carla decided to meet Guy, but called her friend Cathy to let her know the time and place they were going to meet. She had no reason to trust Guy at this point, but really did believe that he was harmless. It turned out that Guy really did have an explanation. His main job was as an undercover agent for the government. The car rental job was just one of the temporary cover jobs that overlapped by a few weeks with his job as a professor at the college. As a matter of fact his final day with the rental company was the day that Carla arrived in San Diego. When he met Carla he was working on the largest case in his young career, and the largest embezzlement case ever in the state of Nevada. The bust was to have happened the following week but because he was there it turned out that everything came together and they were able to execute the sting at that time. Carla remembered hearing about that case in the news after she returned from Las Vegas. He showed her his government ID displaying Top Secret Security Clearance. Guy had been on an assignment. He actually had a copy of a picture from surveillance that his coworkers had put on his desk as a joke. He was the brunt of jokes in his office. The picture revealed that the infamous *Las*

Vegas kiss was on the side of the mouth. Guy explained that nothing like that had ever happened on his job before, and that he was not at liberty to explain any more.

Guy was expected to work in the eastern region for at least the next three years and expressed to Carla that he wanted to spend as much time as possible with her. He said that he would be patient, but would understand if she was unable to forgive him.

After a few weeks and more evidence and convincing, Carla came around and began to see Guy again.

Things were good for Carla in her personal life and at Erie Technical for the next several months, so she enjoyed it all while it lasted.